Jake Kincannon, PI

Across the Sea of Time

Jw Grodt

JAKE KINCANNON, PI
ACROSS THE SEA OF TIME

iUniverse books may be ordered through booksellers or by contacting:

iUniverse
1663 Liberty Drive
Bloomington, IN 47403
www.iuniverse.com
1-800-Authors (1-800-288-4677)

Because of the dynamic nature of the Internet, any web addresses or links contained in this book may have changed since publication and may no longer be valid. The views expressed in this work are solely those of the author and do not necessarily reflect the views of the publisher, and the publisher hereby disclaims any responsibility for them.

ISBN: 978-1-4917-4550-2 (sc)
ISBN: 978-1-4917-5390-3 (hc)
ISBN: 978-1-4917-4549-6 (e)

Library of Congress Control Number: 2014915356

Print information available on the last page.

iUniverse rev. date: 08/20/2015

CONTENTS

PROLOGUE

1977

I was in search of a murder weapon used to brutally kill several young women in Wyoming. I was convinced I knew the location of the murder weapon and the murderer. I waited until dark and drove over to the location where I was sure I would find it. I parked across the road from the Farley farm and walked stealthily down the long driveway toward the house. I stopped near a large oak to conceal myself as I took time to survey the terrain. I was roughly three hundred feet from Rick Farley's shop, and I was concerned about dogs; they could give me away—or worse. So I waited and listened for a moment. I saw lights only on the second floor of the white-frame farmhouse, but Farley's shop was dark, and there were no dogs around that I could see or hear. Since the wind was at my back, if there had been dogs on the premises, they should have picked up my scent and begun barking by now.

After about ten minutes, the lights on the second floor went out, and all was quiet. I waited for another ten minutes or so to be sure that the coast was clear, and then I carefully and quietly moved toward the shop. I was surprised and pleased that the shop door wasn't locked. Once inside, I pulled a small flashlight from my pocket to search for the murder weapon I was certain was there. It didn't take long before I found it wrapped in a towel and hidden in a large wooden box under a tractor tire. I was fascinated by it. What an ingenious killing tool, a set of modified hedge trimmers. The formerly useful, very common hand tool had been converted into something with one intention: brutal and heinous murder. Someone, most likely Farley, had taken a pair of hedge trimmers, broken off the points of the blades, and then heated and twisted the tips 90 degrees from their original position. Then this madman, the creator of this weapon, had taken two steel straps, each one and a half inches wide, and bent each into a U-shape. He had then cut pieces of steel dowel rods, milled one end of each piece to a softly rounded point, and then welded the other end to the two steel straps like teeth. He even made them so they would fit together when closed, like the teeth and jaws of an animal. I was amazed by the ingenuity and skill that had gone into fashioning such a deadly and cruel weapon. Guns and hammers had uses other than taking human life, but this tool had only one purpose. That sole purpose was to kill people. I knew at that instant I had solved the identity of the Werewolf Killer.

It even had the one missing tooth. I held the piece of metal that had been found in the latest victim's neck up to it, and it was a perfect match. The coroner was one of this small town's two doctors and not very experienced in this role. However, the town had little use for a coroner, and he hadn't thought it was related to the crime; that's how I was able to get it. There was no doubt that this was the murder weapon. No question about it. These choppers went from chopping hedges to chopping people. My plan was to place this weapon of horror back where I found it, bring the police back with a warrant to search the premises, and find the weapon. The police would arrest Rick Farley, and a blood test would likely seal his fate. I would have solved the crime and would collect my reward as promised. Julie and I would return to Chicago with plenty of money to fund our agency for quite some time. Little did I know that everything I had been thinking was about to go terribly wrong.

As I was ready to leave and notify the police, I suddenly felt a sharp, horrible pain in the back of my skull. Someone—I didn't know who at that particular moment—hit me with something from behind, not hard enough to turn out the lights but damn near. I dropped the weapon and stumbled forward as I tried to keep myself upright. Gravity won out, however, and I dropped to my knees and turned my head in time to see it was Farley coming at me again with a short club in his hand. He swung wildly, catching me on the shoulder and knocking me down again. I struggled to get to my feet. He spotted and grabbed his killing weapon and began to growl loudly like a dog or wolf as he lunged at me again. The snapping of the metallic jaws of his weapon grew closer before I could get to my feet. When he was close enough, I used my legs to kick him in the gut, and he slammed back into the opposite wall.

I quickly got to my feet, fear pumping through my body, adrenaline rushing. I grabbed the closest thing I could find—a short club beside me—and I went for him with it. He ducked to the side and swung his closed weapon, hitting my hands and causing me to drop the club. He quickly opened the jaws and went for my face. I raised my arm quickly and felt the cold steel teeth rip into the flesh of my forearm. Blood soaked through my sleeve, and pain shot through my body. Anger swelled in me, and I hit him square between the eyes with my right fist.

Blood poured from my left arm as he stumbled backward, trying to catch his balance before his feet went out from under him. He fell, striking his head on a post, rendering him unconscious. I looked around quickly, flipped on the light switch, grabbed a short hunk of rope from the workbench, and used my right hand and teeth to tie a tourniquet around my arm above my wound. While I struggled to stop the bleeding, I didn't notice him come to and sneak up behind me, the weapon in his hands. At the last second, I saw his shadow on the wall and moved quickly to my right. I moved quickly enough to save my life but not fast enough to avoid another vicious wound. This time, my upper chest felt the steel. Fortunately my jacket kept the weapon from sinking deep enough to inflict a fatal wound. He was quick, and before I could punch him again, he opened the homemade jaws, revealing its many teeth, and lunged for my throat again. My reflexes caused me to once again raise my left arm in a defensive movement, and that's when he clamped the weapon around the inside of my upper arm. I felt pain as the steel sunk slightly into my flesh again, but he stopped to a holding position. I froze and stood motionless. If he squeezed the handles together or I tried to pull away, this time he would tear the brachial artery running down the inside of my arm, and I would bleed out in seconds. I had never felt so helpless in my life as he stared into my eyes, his gaze darting back and forth from one of my eyes to the other as if he was searching for something. He said nothing, just continued softly growling, much like a dog when it tries to stare you down. His nose wrinkled up, and he bared his teeth. He almost looked like a werewolf, save the lack of a hairy face and huge canine teeth, but he had teeth all right—man-made and deadly—and now they were buried in my flesh, rendering me unable to move without risking certain death. What could save me now?

However, a waitress I met in 1937 saved me—momentarily at least from a horrific and most real memory.

Now look what I've done; I have confused you terribly. You're probably wondering how I captured a killer in 1977 and was rescued by this waitress I met in 1937? Let me take you back to where it all began, and you'll see why the answer to this riddle makes this case the most bizarre adventure and one that only a suicidal idiot would have accepted.

CHAPTER 1

MY GAL FRIDAY

1977

I'm Jake Kincannon, and I was, and still am, a private investigator. This is my story, and while the case of the Werewolf Killer, as the media dubbed it, was incredible, it was far from the strangest case I would ever work to date. This case and what happened to me, you'll likely find unbelievable. But I can assure you it did happen.

A part of my story involves the age-old struggle between the sexes, as do most stories. I suppose all stories worth repeating do, down through the ages—like Adam and Eve, Samson and Delilah, Julius Caesar and Cleopatra, Romeo and Juliet, Bonnie and Clyde, Frankie and Johnny, and countless more. More stories than there are stars in the heavens. From great love stories that have brought a tear to one's eye and end in romantic bliss, to the love tragedies and triangles that all too often end with someone's divorce or demise, and those of missed opportunities and unrequited love. My story isn't so different in that regard, except this is a story that had a twist I won't ever forget, and I suspect that after you hear my tale, neither will you.

The bicentennial year for the US of A was over. It was a beautiful summer in Chicago as the United States entered its third century as a country. Compared to other nations, we were relatively young. It was also the beginning of my private practice and is the beginning of my story.

I remember that it was a Friday, just past lunchtime, and I was sitting at the large mahogany desk in the reception area of my new office suite. The combined smell of the fresh paint on the walls and doors and the freshly refinished, blond hardwood floors still hung in the air. A man had just finished lettering one side of the solid glass, double-door entry to my suite, so they were propped open. The lettered sign on the glass read:

Jake Kincannon, PI
Private Investigations
Specializing in the Paranormal

I'd had to open all the windows in order not to pass out from the fumes, thus allowing the noise of cars and commuter trains from the busy Chicago streets below to infiltrate my brain. These sounds were so familiar to me that they were not the least bit distracting. The pictures that I had purchased earlier were resting on the floor in the locations below where I thought they would eventually be hung. The hardwood floors glistened in the sunlight that streamed through the open windows and danced across them, adding to the newness of my humble establishment. I was making a list of needed office supplies when I heard a slight tap on the jamb of my open doors. I looked up as she walked toward me on the red rosin paper left by the floor finishers to protect the curing finish.

"Excuse me, sir. I'm looking for Mr. Kincannon?"

"Yes, that would be me. How may I help you, miss?" I wondered if this could possibly be my first client. But she seemed too young to need my services.

"I've come in response to your newspaper advertisement for the girl Friday position."

Yes, I know. Perhaps not a politically correct job title, but it does encompass all the usual position titles in a larger company—receptionist, secretary, office manager, bookkeeper, errand girl, and lunch fetcher—all rolled into one person, a girl Friday. Seems folks are carrying that politically correct stuff a bit too far for my taste.

I remember looking up and thinking, somewhat jokingly, *Wow. If she's half as smart as she is gorgeous, she's hired.* It wasn't just that she was beautiful; there was something about her that struck me instantaneously, something special, an aura if you will. I was only beginning to get some inkling of just how special all her qualities were. My detective's brain quickly compiled her physical structure: five foot seven; midtwenties; blonde hair; blue eyes; flawless, silky, milky-white skin; an hourglass figure; well-developed calves, perhaps a dancer or athlete. Her hose were called Nude, just enough color in them to make those beautiful legs look ever so slightly tanned. She wore her hair up, but I could tell it was long. Her nails were a muted shade of red that matched her lipstick. Her makeup was applied lightly, and it almost appeared as though she didn't wear any.

"Why yes, come in and have a seat," I said, trying to sound and act employerish. Her walk appeared to be one of confidence, not arrogance or conceit. Her clothes were tasteful yet conservative. Her black skirt was just long enough that when she sat down, it completely covered her knees. She sat with her knees and ankles together and her legs tilted slightly to her left. She held her head up and her back straight, and she clutched the leather folder in her lap with both hands.

She smiled, retrieved a paper from her folder, and handed it to me. "Sir, here's my résumé. I know I'm short on experience, but I learn fast, I'm organized, and I want to show someone that I can do a good job. Frankly, I've only applied for jobs I knew I could do well. I'd be happy to answer any questions you may have, sir."

She folded her hands in her lap after handing me the résumé and sat quietly without fidgeting.

"Give me just a moment to read this, Miss … Miss Carson, is it?"

"Yes, sir. Julie Carson."

I peeked up periodically and watched her glance around the room as I read the résumé. It said she could type and take dictation, and I could hear that her voice was certainly pleasant to the ear and her grammar was that of an English teacher. Her résumé was well written and easy to read, as it had very little on it. She continued to sit there almost motionless, save the slight turning of her head and eyes to observe my office layout. She was obviously schooled in appropriate behavior and dress. As she said, though, she was definitely short on experience.

"Miss Carson, you are short on experience, I see, and as you stated."

"Yes, sir. That seems to be all I hear." She hung her head.

It seemed to me that she might be a good fit for me, and she wasn't asking for too much in salary. So I said, "But then how does one get experience if no one will give that person a chance?"

Her head came up with a smile. "Oh, Mr. Kincannon, I'm not afraid of hard work, and I'm willing to work overtime if needed, and—"

"Miss Carson, when are you available to start … should you be offered the position, I mean."

She took a deep breath and replied, "Why, I could start Monday."

"Oh dear, I'm sorry. I'm afraid that won't work for me. No, not at all …" I faked a look of disappointment and watched her smile depart again. Then a puzzled look came across her pretty face until I said, "I need someone today!"

Her smile quickly returned. "Oh, sir, that's not a problem. I'm ready, and I would gladly start today, right this second if you wish!"

"I wish." I stood, extended my hand, and said, "Miss Julie Carson, welcome aboard."

"Oh, thank you, sir!"

With that, she jumped up and shook my outstretched hand quite vigorously. It made me chuckle inside. I felt quite fortunate, as my instincts told me I had found someone special right away. I thought that perhaps this was even an omen of good fortune. However, I had no idea at that particular moment just how special!

"Now, you did say right this second, didn't you?"

"Oh, yes, sir, yes, sir!"

I moved out from behind the desk and gestured for her to sit. "Welcome to your desk. May you be together for a very long time."

Once seated, she held up her crumpled employment section of the paper. "Sir, would you like me to call the newspaper and cancel this help-wanted advertisement?"

"Julie, I think that would be an excellent idea. Also, I finished a list of office supplies, and you may go down to the stationary store on the corner and pick them up."

"Yes, sir."

"Oh, and when you return, could you see if you can do something with those pictures?"

"Absolutely, sir."

"Hmm … by the way, if you want to keep this job, you'll drop all that *sir* business and call me Jake, except in front of clients, of course." I sent her a smile and a wink at the end of my statement to let her know I was playing.

"Oh, of course … Jake." She returned the smile as if to acknowledge my meaning, and I headed for my desk while she jumped right into her tasks.

Julie was obviously my first and only girl Friday, and I suspect it will stay that way as long as I can keep the doors open or someone from stealing her away from me. The interesting thing is that it was a Friday, and just like Robinson Crusoe found his man on a Friday and then so named him, so was it for me. When I started to talk about that story with Julie, she informed me that she had to read that book for a report in high school. I would occasionally call her that in a somewhat tongue-in-cheek manner.

CHAPTER 2

MY NEW BOSS

Julie Carson—that's what it read on the mailbox door, my mailbox door. One of several hundred mailboxes located in the alcove at the rear of the lobby and to the left of the elevators. It was Friday evening around seven when I walked into the lobby of my apartment building and to my mailbox. I liked seeing my name on it, Julie Carson. It made me feel independent, like an adult, like I had my own identity, not just somebody's daughter. I opened it with pride and retrieved my one piece of mail, hopped on the elevator, and soon walked through my apartment door. Once it was closed behind me, I threw my things in the air and twirled around in excitement. I was feeling rather proud of myself that I, Miss Julie Carson, born and raised in Martins Ferry, Ohio, one of the many little steel mill towns along the Ohio River, graduate of Martins Ferry High School, now living in Chicago, was now the assistant to Mr. Jake Kincannon, the tall, handsome private investigator. I got the job, but I could hardly believe it. I had to call home and share my news with Mom and Dad. I dialed their number and listened to each ring, hoping they were home, and breathed a sigh of relief when finally I heard a click and, "Hello?"

"Hi, Mom. How are you?"

"Well, hello, Julie, darling. I'm fine. In fact, your father and I were just discussing you at dinner and wondering if you would call tonight. How have you been, sweetie?"

"I'm great, Mom. Really great. And guess what … I got a job, a real full-time job!"

"Really? Why, that's wonderful, darling. Tell me all about it. No … wait. Hold on a sec. Let me get your father to the other phone so he can hear the good news also. Bill, it's our daughter! Please pick up the extension! She has something to tell us!"

"Okay, dear," I heard Dad say in the background, and I waited for and heard the click of the extension, "Hello, Julie. How's my favorite daughter?"

"Fine, Dad, but I'm your only daughter."

"I know, but you'd still be my favorite even if I had a dozen."

"Bill, stop fooling around. Julie has something special to tell us."

"Yes, dear. What is it, Julie?"

"Dad, I got a job today!"

"Great, Julie! That's just great!"

"Come on, dear. Out with the details," Mom said impatiently.

"Well, I was sitting at this little outdoor café today, having some coffee and a bite to eat while I searched through the help-wanted ads and circled the ones that sounded good. I had been on a dozen interviews this morning and yesterday. But nobody wanted me because of my lack of experience. I must admit I was getting pretty discouraged. Anyway, I was sitting there when I saw an ad for a girl Friday with a private investigator's office. I had circled about half a dozen ads, but this one gave the address, and I realized the office was in the building directly across the street. So I decided to just go over in hopes that perhaps I could get a face-to-face interview."

"You mean you just went there without an appointment, bold as brass?"

"Yes, Mom, I did."

Dad chuckled. "Good for you, Julie. Way to go, young lady."

"I was just tired of the rejections, so I summoned my courage and marched into the office. And this really handsome man was sitting there at the reception desk. At first I thought perhaps he had gotten the job, but it turned out to be the owner. When I told him why I was there, I was worried that he would tell me he had already hired someone or to submit my résumé or I wasn't experienced enough or something. But he looked at my résumé on the spot and asked me when I could start. I told him Monday, but he told me that just wouldn't work. Oh, Mom, Dad, I was so disappointed, and then he looked up at me, smiled, and said he needed someone today, right that minute! I told him I could do it, jumped up, and shook his hand before he could change his mind. That's it. That's how it happened. So now I work for Jake Kincannon, private investigator."

"Julie, that's wonderful. Just wonderful. I'm so proud of you! So, has he been in business long?"

"No, Dad. Actually, he just started his business. In fact, after he hired me, he had me finish the office supply order that he had started, and then he had me hang up the pictures that were lying around the office. It was a good thing too, since he had the layout all wrong."

"That's men for ya," Mom said with a chuckle.

"Women! Always blame the men. And so on that note, I'll say good night, sweetie. Take care of yourself, and congratulations on the job. You be sure to call us next week."

"Sure, Dad. I will. Love you!"

"Love you too, sweetie. Goodnight." *Click.*

"So tell me about this guy. What's his name? What do you mean he's handsome? Is he married?"

"Hold on, Mom. One question at a time. His name is Jake Kincannon, as I mentioned. He looks to be about five or six years older than me. He has these dark brown eyes and hair and is probably about six foot two or three. He looks like he played basketball in school. He has several trophies in his office, and he's good-looking, in a rugged sort of way. He has a deep dimple in his chin; it reminds me of the actor you like so much. What's his name?"

"You mean Kirk Douglas."

"Yes, that's the one. He seems nice, and I like the office, and he's paying me slightly more than I asked for on my résumé."

"He didn't try anything funny ... did he?" There was a slightly worried tone in Mom's voice.

"Stop, Mom. No, he didn't. He seems to be a very nice gentleman. Anyway, I can take care of myself, and since you asked, no, he's not married."

"Okay, dear, okay. Sorry I asked."

"It's okay, Mom. You just worry too much."

"Of course I worry; that's my job as a mom. By the way, will you have to drive every day in that big-city traffic?"

"No, there's a commuter train from my apartment to the office ... Oh, Mom, someone's at the door. Must be the pizza man with my dinner. I'll call you next week. Good night. Love you!"

"Good night, dear. Love you too. Bye."

CHAPTER 3

THE WEREWOLF CASE

The next two months went by with no exciting work, but Julie and I had the office ready. All systems were on go. All we needed now were some big-paying clients. One morning I arrived at my office, and before I opened the door, I stopped abruptly when through those glass doors I saw a vision that required an eyeball investigation.

There was the lovely Miss Julie Carson, a.k.a. Friday, stretched across her desk, reaching to pick up some mail. I was glad she hadn't simply walked around the desk to pick it up, as the sight of her red skirt pulled well up around her thighs revealed a bit more of those well-developed legs than I was ever privy to see, and that skirt drawn up tightly against her nicely rounded rear exposed curves pleasing to a man's eyes! I paused quietly for a moment to let my eyes act like the shutter of a camera, clicking off a series of indelible photos to hang forever in the gallery of my mind. My admiration for her extremely shapely body and angelic face was a secret I held close to my vest. I didn't want her to think me a letch—or worse.

Julie was a very attractive woman and had a seductive voice even though I was certain she wasn't trying to be seductive, or maybe that was just my perception. However, it was not just her beauty and physical attributes that I admired. It was also her ability on the job, her friendship and loyalty, her dedication to the success of the firm, and my overall respect for this fine person I had been lucky enough to find.

Time marched on, and weeks turned into months, and months turned into another year. It was early summer again, June 1978 to be exact, the beginning of our second fiscal year. My business was still just sputtering along with those little, uninteresting types of cases that didn't pay much, but I suppose it helped us keep the doors open. I must admit though that I looked forward to the day when I would send those types of cases to some rookie PI down the road. We had made it through the first year, although just barely.

It was Julie who kept me going with her ever-positive confidence that the big-money cases would come. I think I might have closed the doors by that point if not for her. She was as good as I was at getting people in to see me and keeping us going on those little, somewhat distasteful jobs, like chasing down cheating spouses and getting dirt on people for various reasons. It was all perfectly legal and aboveboard, just not my cup of tea. Julie would spend her own money to buy out-of-town newspapers and gather discarded magazines to look for stories about the strange, the unexplained, and the paranormal. These were the kinds of cases I was seeking and hoping to find and make a living from. She occasionally found some, and we would stay late in the office, discussing them and eating carryout food, sometimes working until dawn, making calls throughout the United States and around the world. While we found many potential cases, it seemed that most of the people investigating these types of cases were governments, and they couldn't or wouldn't hire outside investigators. Julie was truly a godsend. She kept trying and kept me trying as well.

Then it happened. It just goes to show you that persistence does pay off. She was following up on a story in a magazine about some bizarre killings. The press had dubbed the perp the Werewolf Killer. According to the magazine article, a man unhappy with the efforts of law enforcement to solve this case, a case involving the brutal death of his youngest of three daughters, had decided to take matters into his own hands. He was now offering a substantial reward, twenty-five thousand to be exact, to anyone who could provide information leading to the arrest of this killer or the elimination of the animal. He had made his money in munitions and had semiretired to a ranch in Wyoming. After his conversation with Julie, he agreed to pay our airfare to come and hear his story and hopefully solve the mystery. It seemed a few people were killed in a very strange way; many believed it to be the doings of a werewolf. The father just wanted justice, and he was willing to pay for it.

When Julie relayed the story to me, I rolled my eyes and told her to call him back and tell him to send us an advance of one thousand dollars, and we would let him know what day we would arrive. A week later, we were on our way from Chicago. Wyoming was experiencing warmer than usual temperatures for early June, which was fine by me. I had visions of freezing my tail feathers off. Good ol' Julie checked that out ahead of time and told me to pack accordingly.

We first landed in Cheyenne and then caught a puddle jumper to Harvey Field in Rawlins. Our new client, Mr. Ray Talbot, picked us up for the two-hour ride to his ranch near the town of Sand Drew, Wyoming. That was how he put it, but the word *near* in Wyoming definitely had a different meaning than it did where we were from. We mostly made small talk on the long, bone-jarring ride until we finally reached the Longhorn Ranch, one thousand acres of various terrains where Mr. Talbot raised longhorn cattle and buffalo. He actually had cowboys that still rode the fence lines and rounded up cattle, but on much smaller terms than most of us remember from the old westerns on TV.

When we arrived, we were shown to our respective rooms and given an opportunity to clean up before supper. By the time we returned downstairs, supper was served, and I for one was glad, as we hadn't eaten much that day, and the smell of beef cooking was tremendous. Mr. Talbot served us some longhorn and buffalo for dinner. Both were excellent. We nibbled around the edges of our reason for being there, but we didn't get into the gist of it until we were having brandy in the study afterward. Now full and relaxing with our drinks, we got into what was going on in the area.

The background was that women were being killed on the nights of the full moon. Our client's daughter was victim number five out of a total of eight so far. Another full moon was on its way. Each victim had her throat ripped out and bite marks and deep lacerations all over her body. The local sheriff was convinced it was a bear or mountain lion. But that didn't withstand the logic test. First, the victims were not eaten; therefore, it was not a case of predation. Yes, bears had been known to kill in defense of their young and leave the victim dead but uneaten. But when confronted by the fact that all the killings had occurred only on nights of the full moon, it was just too coincidental to be any wild animal. The papers, of course, speculated that it was a werewolf. That sold papers, and the killing style did fit the behavior of the legendary Wolf Man. But the sheriff had dismissed the theory of a werewolf as preposterous and merely newspaper propaganda to achieve one thing: selling more papers.

I explained that while I didn't personally believe in werewolves, I did believe that there were people who believed they were werewolves and killed accordingly and that some serial killers liked to disguise their killings as such to help throw police off the trail. I was convinced that it was a "whomever" not a "whatever." But either way, we were confident we would solve the mystery.

"You are welcome here at Longhorn Ranch for as long as you need to solve it."

"Thank you, Ray. We appreciate that."

"I will also have a car for your use, as well as horses whenever you need them. You can ride, I trust?"

"Yes," I said confidently. Julie … well, she wasn't very convincing.

He promised to give us good and gentle steeds. We finished our drinks and retired for the night. Ray informed us that breakfast was served promptly at 0630; come late, go hungry. I could see that Ray was a principled and regimented man, who also used military time. I liked that.

The next morning, we were given maps of the area and keys to the Jeep, and off we went to talk with the sheriff and folks who had firsthand knowledge of anything surrounding the case. I would ask the questions, and Julie would take shorthand notes of their responses.

Now, the sheriff confided in me, off the record, that he thought it was a serial killer, but he continued with the official theory that it was an animal, which was possible but highly improbable. The sheriff was merely trying to prevent more panic than necessary. However, if it was a man or werewolf, he was not looking in the right areas as he was convinced that it was a newcomer or stranger to the area. I was not yet ready to accept that theory, and I was still certain it was a person suffering from lycanthropy or just a clever killer's disguise. And as far as the local media's contention that it was a werewolf, I was not convinced of the existence of werewolves, but I was open to the possibility.

So far, the sheriff's methods had kept the perp safe from capture, so I was determined to capture him, it, or them. It was little over a week until the next full moon, and I wanted to catch this killer before he could strike again. We looked at each victim for commonality with one another. None was apparent. They seemed to be victims of opportunity. These were young women who had just happened to wind up in a wrong-place, wrong-time scenario. Each killing had taken place in a remote area, but then almost everything in Wyoming was remote.

After the first few days went by, we knew the history very well, but we still had no good clues. On the Saturday before the full moon, we went out on horseback with a guide to survey the landscape and visit some of the murder sites. We spent the entire day, from sunrise to sunset, going from site to site. One thing became clear: the murder sites seemed to have a pattern to them. I plotted them on a map as we rode along. That night, we slept under the stars in sleeping blankets. Julie was a bit frightened, so she pulled her blanket next to mine. Our guide fell asleep like this was nothing special, but for us two city folks, it was so beautiful—but also a bit unnerving.

"Julie, did you ever see so many stars?"

"No. I had no idea there were so many. The lights of the city must obscure the smaller stars from sight."

"Yes, I think you're—"

I was interrupted by the howl of a wolf in the distance. It was a chilling sound, at least for big-city folk. Our guide didn't even stir. The wolf just kept howling like he was calling his mate. Each time he howled, Julie wiggled a little closer to me. The scent of her hair was very pleasing. She lifted her head to say something to me, and our lips were suddenly very close. My next move would change our relationship forever.

"Jake, do you—"

I interrupted her query with a kiss. I couldn't help myself. I felt her stiffen as if she would pull away. Then she relaxed and accepted it. We pulled away after the kiss was over and stared into each other's eyes as if to see what had just happened. I wanted to kiss her again. Her lips were warm, soft, and enticing. As I slowly began to move my lips closer to hers once again, she stopped the intense mood by placing her hand softly over my lips.

"No, Jake. I'm unsure of why this happened. Maybe we're star drunk or something."

I had never heard of being star drunk, but I cared too much for her to persist. She said good night and turned her back to me, and I said and did the same. I don't know if she had difficulty, but I had a hard time falling asleep. I pondered why it had happened and what it meant. Little did I know where that night under the stars would lead.

The next morning was more than a little uncomfortable. I woke first, and the millions of stars that had seduced us had melted away with the early morning sunshine. The land was flat and picturesque—a vast, open land speckled with a few trees here and there. It was breathtaking watching the sun come up from the east. I walked over to where our guide, Mac, had already prepared an open fire and was readying to cook up some grub, as he put it. He handed me a tin cup filled with some black coffee.

"How'd ya sleep, Mr. Kincannon?"

I had to contain myself, as what had happened earlier in the night flashed through my mind with his query. "All in all, very well, Mac. Of course the ground as a mattress will take a little getting used to." He chuckled, as did I. "Oh and, Mac, please call me Jake."

"Well, Jake, it looks like the young lady's beginning to stir."

I glanced over my shoulder to see Julie sitting up and rubbing her eyes as if to rub away the sleep. When I turned back, Mac was handing me another cup of joe. "Thanks, Mac."

I walked toward Julie, not sure what I would say, so I kept it simple. "Good morning. Like some coffee?"

She blushed and reached for the cup. As she did, she looked deeply into my eyes for an uncomfortable few seconds. Then she thanked me for the coffee and turned her head away as if ashamed of what had happened. I wanted to say something like it was only a kiss or we didn't have sex. I just didn't want to say something that would make it worse, so I took the cue and walked back to the fire.

Our guide now had prepared eggs and bacon in addition to the coffee. It reminded me of the old westerns I had watched as a kid growing up in the city, but I had never done anything like that myself. Julie finally came over to the fire and was perfectly normal to Mac, but she wouldn't or couldn't bring herself to look at me. Mac served up the food on tin plates, and we ate pretty much in silence.

Finally, when Julie had finished, she asked, "Mac, how do you clean up the dishes out here? Can I help?"

"No, missy. I can take care of it. I'll just wash them quickly in the stream over thataway." He pointed toward some trees.

"May I go there and freshen up first?"

"Sure, missy. Just keep an eye out for snakes. We got rattlers out here."

She seemed to take that comment in stride as she walked toward the stream. Mac dumped the small amount of leftover food into the fire and then went over to where the horses were tied and saddled them. When Julie came back, her hair was pulled back and tied. Her face was fresh and beautiful. What had we done? My fear was that she would quit when we returned. We could hardly look at each other, and we struggled to act as if nothing had happened, but how does one put the genie back in the bottle? Mac poured the leftover coffee over the fire and made sure it was out. Then he walked off with the dishes to the stream.

I walked over to Julie. "Are you okay?"

She turned her back to me. "Yes, I'm fine."

"Look, about last night, I—"

"Jake, I can't talk about it right now. Please."

"Okay, I'm sorry," was all I could think to say. The irresistible urge that had come over me last night, the urge she had surrendered to if only for a brief second, had perhaps changed everything. The urge that had tasted like honey under the star-filled heavens now tasted like vinegar with the dawn, and I didn't know what to say or do.

We didn't speak of it again that day. We worked hard on the case, and soon the night of the full moon was upon us. The sheriff's department and the state police were on high alert, and every officer was out on patrol that night. Julie and I went to the area where I had calculated the next attack would take place. It didn't. We waited all night and left for the ranch at sunrise. We both went straight to our respective rooms, and I went straight to bed. Sleep seemed to come to me as soon as my face hit the pillow.

I was awakened around noon to hear that a victim had been found very near to where we had been staked out all night. The killing had obviously taken place somewhere else, and the body had been transported to that location. This new evidence totally eliminated any possibility that this was the work of an animal. Instead, it confirmed that this was the work of a cunning killer who was positioning the bodies to form the shape of a pentagram on a map.

The nude body of the young woman was covered only in her own blood. There was the same pattern of bite marks and lacerations on her body as with the previous victims, and the cause of death was blood loss from having her throat torn out. Death would have come within seconds of the throat injury, but had the suffering come first or were the other wounds postmortem?

I suggested to the sheriff that the coroner should check to see if this victim had been raped. He resisted at first, out of what seemed to be disbelief on his part. He was used to people being killed by bears, cougars, wolves, and other dangerous predators in this part of the country, but he had never dealt with a serial killer before. Therefore, based on the physical bite marks that tore out the throats of the victims, there didn't seem to be any reason to do such a test. He finally agreed, and as a result of that test, we were now able to conclusively rule out any predation as a cause of death. We kept the part about the victim having been moved out of any reports and left the official cause of death report state that all the victims died as a result of an attack by a bear or other large predator.

Julie and I followed up with the coroner's office the next day and found that the victim had a sufficient quantity of sperm within the vaginal area to determine blood type. We suppressed that tidbit of info as well.

While doing that test, the coroner found something imbedded in the latest victim's flesh that was very interesting—a rounded piece of metal ground to a soft point at the end. The piece of metal was about half an inch long with a rough spot at the top of it. Still another tidbit of information we kept under wraps for the time being. Nobody seemed to think much about that little piece of metal but me. The coroner just mentioned it in passing and said he thought it had probably been picked up from something on the ground as the victim and the perp fought.

I had a different take on it. I asked Ray if they had a blacksmith in town or someone who was a good metalworker. He told me there was a man who had a farm on the other side of town. They used him to repair broken metal tools, miscellaneous farm equipment, and such. He was a very good welder and metalworker. He sounded perfect, so I decided to pay him a visit. I told Julie to stay behind this trip in case he was our perp.

I asked Ray for something he had that was made of metal and worn or broken. We walked to the stable and found a bridle with a broken bit and a pitchfork with two broken teeth.

Without divulging my plan to Ray, I got directions from him to Rick Farley's farm and drove there. I found Rick outside repairing a fence along the driveway near some outbuildings. He was an unusually thin man about six feet tall with long, stringy hair tied back behind his head with a gum band. He had a long scar on the left side of his face; it ran from his hairline almost to his chin. He also had a nervous twitch in his eyes, and he blinked constantly. When we shook hands, his grip was like a vise. I told him of my broken items and asked if he could fix them. He nodded but seemed suspicious of me. I guessed that he must not see many strangers around there. Or was it his guilt that unsettled him?

"Are you new around here, mister?"

"Kincannon, Jake Kincannon. No. I'm an old friend of Ray Talbot's. I'm in town for a week, just visiting him. He said he needed to bring these things to you to fix, so I volunteered in order to save him a trip. He's so busy with his place, you know."

"I see. Yes, I've repaired a lot of things for Mr. Talbot. By the way, what line of work are you in?"

"I'm a real estate broker in Chicago. Have been for fifteen years."

"How's the market back in Chicago?"

"We're having a very good year so far. I think things are finally improving."

He seemed satisfied and assured me that he could repair both items. He asked me to come back late the next afternoon and said they would be ready for me.

As I stood there, I could see the shop where Rick Farley did his metalwork. I was now formulating a plan. I thanked him and told him I would be back the next day around 1500. He said fine, and I left. He knew what time I meant, so he was perhaps ex-military. As I drove away, I didn't see any dogs around, so I planned to come back that night around 2100. That night, I waited until Julie retired before I borrowed Ray's Jeep again and drove back to the Farley place.

This is where my story began, me deep into thoughts of this case as I struggled to regain my memory, when suddenly that cute, young waitress interrupted my trancelike thoughts.

That brawl had ended with me in death's shadow, and we were standing still, both of us breathing hard from the encounter. He had me where I couldn't move. When was he going to finish me? He was toying with me now, like a cat with a mouse in its claws. All he had to do was push the two handles together, back away, and watch me die. I wasn't sure if I should try to talk to him or just pray. There was no way to escape the grip of his homemade werewolf jaws. My mind raced for a solution, but none came. Truly, my whole life flashed before me, but most of my thoughts were of Julie. I knew I would never see her again, and that was the worst of it. Then the standoff changed when suddenly a male voice spoke softly from behind him.

"Son, I can't allow you to kill another person."

Farley snapped his head around to look behind him and then looked back to me. The shocked expression on his face was amazing; it went from that of a wild animal to that of a terrified, whimpering child. He opened the jaws of the weapon, turned and tried to hide it behind his back, again just like a child might do. He now faced the man, who held a double-barrel shotgun pointed right at him. My shaking body slid to the floor. It was a sight to behold—a bearded, old man with one leg missing from the knee down, leaning on an old homemade crutch and holding a shotgun on Farley. He was wrinkled and scruffy in appearance, but he looked like an angel to me. He saved me, at least momentarily. I quickly deduced that this must be Farley's father. Tears poured down the old man's face as his son dropped the weapon and went to his knees before him, crying like a five-year-old about to be punished for some mischievous prank.

"Daddy, I'm sorry. I won't do it again. Please don't hurt me."

"Son, you are my responsibility, and you must sin no more. I can't allow it. The evil that is within you is beyond redemption. I have also sinned, as I couldn't bring myself to believe what in my heart I knew. I must destroy that evil and its maker."

Farley, sensing his father's determination, suddenly changed back into his wolflike character. He jumped to a doglike crouched position and began to growl softly again. Then he lunged for the old man, and the shotgun went off. The blast of buckshot peeled the skin and flesh right off his skull and sent him flying backward. He fell motionless to the floor in a pool of blood.

"God forgive me!" Those were the last words Rick's father uttered as he quickly turned the shotgun on himself.

I tried to get up and stop him but collapsed back to the floor. I was too weak to get up, much less to prevent his suicide. The second barrel exploded in the quiet night air, and he fell, dead before he hit the ground. They lay there—the son, the Werewolf Killer, as he had become known, and his father. Both were dead. I didn't even know his name, but he had surely saved my life. Now I had to get help soon or I would be the third body found. I struggled to my feet, trying to keep as much blood from vacating my body as possible. I stumbled to the house.

"Anyone here?" I yelled as I went through the door.

I searched for a phone and called 911 for the police and an ambulance. Then I sat down in the living room to wait. This was the closest I had ever come to dying, and at that point, I wasn't out of the woods yet. I wrapped my injured arm more tightly around my body and pressed a rag as tightly to my chest wound as I could. The room got blurry, and that was the last thing I remembered.

When I opened my eyes, I was flat on my back in a hospital bed, with Julie sitting beside me. She told me how the doctors and nurses had cleaned me up and stitched me up. It took two pints of blood to get my dipstick back to full. We talked until I fell asleep or passed out, whichever it was, but Julie was able to get me out a couple days later. I was still weak and spent about two weeks at my client's ranch recuperating, with Julie attending to my every need.

After I was healed and back on my feet, I said, "Ray, could I ask one last favor? Could Julie and I borrow the horses? We'd like to sleep out under the stars one last time. We city folks rarely have such an opportunity for such pleasures."

"Why, you bet. Do you want one of my men to guide you?"

"No, I don't think that will be necessary. We've learned our way around pretty well, and we won't be going too far away."

"Fine then. I'll have one of the boys saddle up the two horses you've been riding."

"Thanks, Ray. I'm grateful."

"No, it's me who's grateful to you for ridding us of the monster that killed my baby and for preventing any further tragedy. I'm only sorry for your injuries."

So, late that afternoon as the sun had just begun to set in the western sky, Julie and I rode out toward the mountains in the far distance until dusk. Then we located a nice spot, prepared a campfire, pulled out some beef jerky, and heated up some beans. We ate off metal plates and drank campfire-cooked coffee, just living the "cowboy life." We watched the sun disappear and the stars get brighter and brighter as the sky became darker and darker. But that night we talked under the stars and the moon and spoke of why we shouldn't start a romantic relationship. We had been employer and employee. We were now very close friends as well, and the future for us and for the business looked bright. We convinced each other that we would resist the yearnings of our emotions. That night, we kept each other warm, wrapped in each other's arms without any romantic interludes. I controlled my strong feelings, and she was now comfortable in my arms and didn't have to have her back to me. I didn't sleep much that night; I guess it was the excitement about solving the case and the check for twenty-five thousand that was in my wallet. Or perhaps it was Julie snuggled in my arms, her scent in my nostrils and the speculation of where we were headed romantically … or not.

CHAPTER 4

YEARS OF LEAN

We returned to Chicago and went back to work, but work would never be the same as it had been before our trip to Wyoming. We worked together, more committed to each other than before, but in a nonromantic way, or so we tried to believe. The funny thing was that we were one of those rare couples that could work together and spend a fair amount of time together socially without damaging one relationship or the other.

We continued to take small jobs, the kind PIs often have to do to survive, but after another year slipped away, we'd had no other good cases like the one that had brought us to a different place. We still followed stories and made calls, but we got nothing. When we joked about it, we said that we'd live on beans and a pine float. We did that all right—a little job here, a little job there, just enough to keep us going until our next big case. We even decided to give up her apartment, and she moved in with me, strictly to save money, we told each other. She had her room, and I had mine. We did it for financial, not romantic reasons, although I was game—she need only give me a hint. None came.

Nineteen seventy-nine was winding down, and she invited me home to spend the Christmas holiday with her and her folks. At first I refused, thinking it wasn't a good idea, but she didn't want me to be alone for the holidays, so she pestered me until I agreed. We drove down to their home in Ohio and spent about five days with them. Little did we know as we drove there that the end of our relationship as we knew it was about to happen.

They were great folks, and they seemed fond of me as well, at least that was what Julie told me. There wasn't much to see in the little town; the steel mills were beginning their slow descent into history. Those plants had provided work for most of the people who called the town home. Some of the first closed plants were skeletons of a dying era. Julie's father, Bill, said he remembered when he was a young man seeing those mills running three shifts a day. Near every gate of these plants was a diner, open 24/7. One group of men would be having breakfast in their clean work clothes while men with dirty clothes and faces were relaxing with cold beers after a hard day's work. However, they were great people, those men who worked the steel that was the backbone of a nation. Julie's father got a little misty-eyed as he talked about it.

During my stay with her folks, we ate well. Mary, Julie's mom, was an excellent cook. We sat around a big fireplace in the living room, drank eggnog, and I enjoyed, *really* enjoyed, the conversation and the ambience. The house was an interesting one. It sat in the side of a hill on a one-acre lot that sloped from the brick-paved street below and then sloped upward to an old abandoned road behind the property. Bill, her dad, told me that when he bought it, it was an abandoned frame house that the town referred to as a haunted house. Mary had not been very happy with his choice of a home, but he renovated it with a sandstone veneer exterior, a two-car garage, and two huge picture windows, one in the living room and one in the dining room. Every room in the house was large with high ceilings.

Our second day there, it snowed about five inches, and the view from the living room window was spectacular. You could look down the hill to the town below and even see parts of the Ohio River.

Their tradition was to get up early on Christmas morning, have pumpkin pie and coffee, and sit around the tree with a nice fire going while waiting for the signal from Mom to open presents. The night before, Christmas Eve, we had a fine meal and sipped brandy with our mincemeat pie in front of the fire. I couldn't remember a time like this since I was a kid, before I lost my parents. Her parents were wonderful and made me feel like family. We talked and laughed until about midnight and then finally went to bed. I must admit, I would have been proud to be part of that family. I wonder if Julie knew how I felt.

Funny thing about Christmas Eve—I still think I hear sleigh bells on the roof as I try to fall asleep. It's the craziest thing.

It must have been about 0200 when I was awoken by a soft knock at my door, and then the dim light from the hallway invaded my room. The light then disappeared as someone closed the door. For a split second, I wasn't sure if someone had come in or had just looked in on me. Then I heard a soft voice say, "I'm yours if you want me."

I knew exactly who it was, and as she passed by the window, I saw her. I wasn't sure if I was dreaming until I felt her sit on the side of the bed and inhaled that fresh but light scent of her soap that I knew all too well. I sat up, and her hand softly touched my shoulder. Without another word, I gently peeled the sheer robe from her body, wrapped her in my arms, and allowed the bedcovers to swallow us up. Not a word was spoken; our bodies carried the conversation. An hour later, she slipped away as quietly as she had appeared.

The next morning, she blushed slightly when our eyes first met, but there wasn't the same kind of uncomfortable feeling we had experienced in Wyoming. We both seemed to understand the deep implications. I wondered what had brought her to me and made her give up her innocence. Was it her parents' approval of me that she had been waiting for? There would be much to discuss, but for now it was time to enjoy the day with her and her family, of which I was now certain I would soon be a part. We had a most wonderful Christmas, including the traditional exchanging of gifts after pie, coffee, and pleasant conversation. Then we dressed for church. They attended a small Lutheran church and introduced me to the pastor prior to the service. He was a most interesting man. He had an eye affliction and blinked constantly. It almost looked painful, and I felt sorry for him. After the songs and prayers, he took the podium. He looked out among the parishioners, and his eyes were like beacons calling out God's message. His eyes didn't blink anymore than mine did. It made me feel that God truly spoke through him. We stayed two days beyond Christmas with her folks and then returned to Chicago to celebrate the New Year our way.

Year four, 1980, started off pretty much like every other year. However, this was the year that there was a surge in UFO sightings. Some were explained away as reflections off airline dashboards, some were hoaxes, and some had real possibilities. But with all our efforts, we could not get a paying gig to prove or disprove them. These alleged sightings also started a new wave of conspiracy theories about the Roswell, New Mexico, incident of 1947. Fortunately, we again had enough small cases to keep it worthwhile to continue. The hard work and struggle to find my kind of cases just made Julie and me closer and more determined. However, as winter months melted into spring, I became increasingly restless at the lack of work, and Julie was having a more and more difficult time keeping me motivated to go on. I was really beginning to contemplate closing the agency, but Julie said she would get a job at the bank, and we would continue to work evenings to find some better cases. I found that thought really distasteful.

On a personal note, we had a pregnancy scare during the spring of that year. We had just about resigned ourselves to becoming premature parents. So after two months, we decided we had better get a professional opinion. We talked a lot about getting married and parenting during those two months, and while we wanted to get the business going before getting married and having kids, we agreed we wanted both. The doctor then informed us that Julie was not pregnant, and he gave us some complicated medical mumbo-jumbo reason for why she was late. He said it wasn't all that uncommon and assured us we were not soon-to-be parents. It was a relief, yet we were both a little down upon hearing the news.

On the third of June 1980, we celebrated the birthday of our business and our meeting. Another year with few prospects for big cases was in sight, and my enthusiasm was fading fast.

They say things happen for a reason, and sometimes when the timing is right, salvation comes along. I was about to get a taste of that.

CHAPTER 5

REFLECTION TIME

I was sitting at my desk one morning a week later, having my usual morning cup of coffee, when Julie buzzed me to say someone was on the phone. He wouldn't give his name, but he said he was an old friend.

"I'll take it."

When I answered the phone, it was an old high school friend— Spencer T. Baxter, Buzz to me and the other kids in school. It seemed he and his wife were in town on a business trip for a few days and wanted to have dinner with me. I told him of Julie, and he invited her as well. She declined, saying I should spend some time with my friend. Besides, she said, she had some things to do that she hadn't been able to do with me around. I made excuses for her and agreed to go alone, thinking it was just a reunion of sorts.

At dinner, we had a nice time talking, telling stories, and laughing. It was a most delightful time, and I hadn't laughed that much in years, but after we got through the three-course dinner and when we were sipping some brandy, he dropped a bomb on me. He offered me a job. Had he known things were slow with my business? Did he just want to show me how well he was doing? Or was he genuinely in need of a good detective? By the time we finished dessert and coffee, he convinced me it was the latter. When it came time to leave, Buzz grabbed the check, and we said our good-byes. I promised to get back with him really soon with an answer and agreed to give his really generous offer serious consideration.

I decided to go back to the office and gather my thoughts before going home and letting Julie know of the offer. As I approached my office door and slipped the key into the lock, I read the name, my name, on the large glass door. I remembered when those words were painted on the glass four years ago. I chuckled to myself and wondered if I had made the right decision to leave my former employ as a gold-shielded homicide detective. I flipped the light switch as I closed the door behind me. I continued to reminisce, standing there and looking at Julie's desk. Then I walked to the window and stared out at Chicago by dark and continued to roll the thoughts and choices around and around in my head. Make the choice to continue to slug it out here with my own company or take the easier and perhaps more profitable one by hooking up with Buzz and accepting his very generous offer of employment.

Sure, I had the money my mother left me, which helped keep me afloat, some money we had saved from our two decent cases, and a full pension thanks to a well-timed Reduction in Force. The department had offered a full retirement for anyone with more than ten years in, so I had jumped at it. I could have stayed with Chicago PD for another ten years and continued to draw a steady paycheck. However, I had always wanted to be a private investigator. Now that I had it, I was beginning to have my doubts.

I'd had visions of it being a very busy and profitable operation. It hadn't played out that way, and the last four years had really tested my mettle. I loved the *Star Trek* TV series of the late sixties. In one episode, the logical Mr. Spock made one of his famous quotes that seems apropos here. He said, "After a time, you may find that having is not so pleasing a thing after all as wanting. It is not logical, but it is often true."

Is this where I've come, to a low point of throwing in the towel? I found that thought in and of itself repugnant. Had it not been for Julie, I think I might have already done just that. I turned back and looked over at her desk and thought, *I can't and won't make this decision without her. She's every bit a part of this as I am.* But before I told her, I had to decide which way I wanted to go. She and I were anxious to marry and start a family. This new job offer would allow us to do that. Continuing the agency would push those plans off into the distant future.

I hung my hat and trench coat on the coat tree near the glass doors, walked into my office, closed the door without turning on the light, and walked over to my big, wooden desk. I sat down in my high-back leather chair and opened the bottom drawer. Then I pulled out my bottle of bourbon and a glass and poured a double. I scoffed as I thought, *This used to always be Jack Daniels. Now it's whatever is the cheapest—self-inflicted punishment for not doing well in the business.* I took a big pull of my drink and felt the bourbon burn as it slid down my pipes. Then I kicked back, propped my feet on the corner of the desk, folded my hands behind my head, leaned back, and stared at the ceiling.

I needed to do some real soul-searching and be brutally honest with myself. I had to reexamine my decision to specialize in my type of investigative work. You'll remember that there was something else written on my door that read, *Specializing in the paranormal.* I was now beginning to think that perhaps my scope of work should have been broadened. Perhaps, as I had once learned in a business course I took, I had "defined myself too narrowly." That was certainly one option: to broaden the scope of my type of work. Then there was my friend's offer. He wanted me to be one of his detectives, working his insurance-fraud cases, for which he would pay me handsomely and provide an expense account. I would even be based in Chicago. It sounded good, and it was another option. The third option, maybe to some the least attractive, was to slug it out with my present business. I knew that would likely be Julie's choice, but she was young and idealistic.

My office was in the rear corner of the building, and directly behind my building was the old Mission Church, one of the oldest buildings in town. It had even survived Mrs. O'Leary's cow. It had been later renovated in 1946. It seemed that this part of town had just grown up around the old church, but they continued to run it. The building had a huge, lighted cross that blinked off and on at night. I had never sat in my office at night without turning on the lights, and as such, I didn't realize how much light came flooding into my office from that blinking sign. It bathed the wall as though a dim light was on, and then it would go out. It was like someone flipping a light switch on and then off and then back on again. The rhythmic pattern of *light, no light, light* was relaxing, but then I noticed something I hadn't noticed before.

"There are huge cobwebs in the corner of my ceiling!" I said aloud, and then I began to laugh. I had the same thing in my business bank account—cobwebs where the big bucks should have been.

"Funny, I never noticed those cobwebs before." Continuing to talk to myself, I said, "Guess I'll have to do something about that … tomorrow … maybe."

So, as the lights from the church continued to chase away the darkness and let it return, I continued to ponder my future as a PI. Perhaps I should have stayed with the department after all. I had been a pretty damn good cop. During those years as a gold shield, I was lead detective on fifty-five cases; fifty-one were solved, four went cold and were shelved, and forty-three were convictions. You can thank the liberal court system for the eight cases where the bad guy or gal got away.

I took another swig of my cheap bourbon and began to relive my time there from day one. I hired Julie, my gal Friday, when I first opened, and she turned out to be quite good and had stuck with me through the rough times, even before our romance started. She even had wanted to give back her paycheck a time or two, but I would not allow that, so I continued to subsidize my own business. Now we had become a couple. That also had to be considered.

I sat there watching the cobwebs appear and disappear with the flashing light and move in a rippling fashion from the light breeze that came through my slightly open window. I decided that the cobwebs fit in well with my office décor. Sitting there alone, I finally concluded that with Julie's help, it was worth forging ahead.

When I returned home, Julie was already asleep, so I waited until the morning, and we discussed it over coffee and on our drive to the office. She was dead set on making a go of it. She told me something interesting: "Love, quitting can become a habit. It's a habit we don't need. If you can so easily give up on the agency that you've dreamed of owning and building since you were a child, maybe you can as easily give up on me."

"Wow!" That was all I could say. I had to ponder that awhile.

When we were inside the office, she kissed me and then said, "I love you, and I know you'll do the right thing." Then she kissed me again.

I grabbed her and kissed her, not a peck, but a full-blown passionate kiss, and then after I cleared my throat and regained a little composure, I said, "Are there any messages?"

"Well, let me catch my breath and call the service."

I went to my office and placed a call to my old friend Buzz. I conveyed my deep appreciation for his very generous offer, but said that Julie and I had discussed it at great length and had finally concluded that we would stay with our agency. As soon as I hung up, my lovely Julie was standing in the doorway.

"Yes. There were three messages. First, Mrs. Tatum called. I returned her call, and she was complaining about the bill we just sent her. She was most anxious to speak to you, but I convinced her that the invoice was correct. The plumber who was here last week wants to know when we're going to pay him for the work he did. I also called him and told him by the end of the month, as his invoice stated. And lastly, a Dr. Wilson J. Wells called. He wouldn't say what it was in reference to, just that it was most urgent and that you should call as soon as you arrive."

As she handed me the notes, I grabbed the phone to call this Dr. Wells. A call I would come to regret making many times.

CHAPTER 6

A VERY STRANGE MEETING

I hoped he was calling because he was in need of my services. The phone rang twice, and then a strange and seemingly somewhat irritated voice demanded, "Yes, what is it?"

"Dr. Wells, my name is Jake Kincannon, private investigator. You called me earlier. How may I help you, sir?"

His tone changed, and his voice became pleasant. "Oh yes, Mr. Kincannon. Thank you for your quick response. I must meet with you right away, at once. Do you have some time?"

"Why yes. I'm in my office. When would you like to stop by?"

"Oh no, you misunderstand. I need you to come to my laboratory, as I have something very important to show you, and it can't be moved."

"Well, that is rather unusual. Can you tell me how I may be of service?"

He became quickly annoyed again and sternly said, "Mr. Kincannon, it is extremely important that I see you immediately, and when you get here, I will explain everything! I will also pay you a five-hundred-dollar advance if you take my case." Now he was talkin' my language!

"Very well. Give me your address, and I'll leave shortly."

At last, another job! It had been a near a month since I billed a job, and that client had just complained about it. I wrote down his address and damn near ran over Julie as she was bringing me my usual cup of coffee. I took a few slugs of it as I told her where I was going. Then, in my excitement, I handed her my cup back, shook her lovely hand, and ran out the door. She must have thought me crazy, as I hadn't shook her hand since I hired her. We were more accustomed to me kissing her as I had done just moments ago.

I had no idea just how radically my life was about to be altered that day, the day I met Dr. Wilson J. Wells, a PhD in science and higher mathematics. He was also an inventor. It was June 12, 1980. It all started that day. It was a day I would never forget, as it was the same month I had started the agency four years ago. Maybe this also was an omen.

Interestingly, the good doctor's office was on the same street as mine, only three buildings to the east, so I decided to just walk there. The building was forty stories tall, a beautiful art-deco-styled building that was built during the time period known as the Roaring Twenties. Yet when I checked the directory, I was surprised to find that there was no Dr. Wells on it. I found that a bit odd, but I got into the elevator anyway; since it had an elevator operator, perhaps he knew which floor I was supposed to go to. I was surprised to see they still actually had an elevator operator, also reminiscent of a much earlier era.

"What floor, sir?"

When I told him I needed the floor of Dr. Wilson J. Wells, he then asked me my name. Now that was a very strange and atypical query. However, it had been a very strange morning anyway, so I shrugged my shoulders and told him. He then picked up the elevator phone and dialed.

"Pardon me, sir. There is a Mr. Jake Kincannon here to see you." He paused and then continued, "Yes, sir. Right away, sir!"

He hung up and immediately closed the cage door. He then pulled a brass key hooked to a gold chain from his watch pocket and slipped it into the elevator panel. When he turned the key, a button located at the bottom of the panel lit up with the letter T. That usually meant terrace level; I figured his office was located on the terrace level—a better-sounding name for the basement. He pushed that button, and as the elevator lurched downward, I thought, *This place is locked up tighter than Fort Knox.* When the elevator stopped and the doors opened, I stepped out into a lab of considerable size. A man was waiting.

"Mr. Kincannon?"

"Yes, sir. Are you Dr. Wells?"

"I am indeed. Thank you for coming so promptly."

When we shook hands, I was surprised by the firmness of his grip.

The good Dr. Wells was as strange looking as everything else I knew about him so far, including his place. He looked to be in his late sixties or early seventies, but he seemed very spry for that age. He wore a long, white smock, brown slacks, and tennis shoes with black socks. His eyes were a bright, piercing blue, and he had very bushy, blond eyebrows. He wore round, thin, wire glasses, which were parked on the bridge of his nose. His messed-up blond hair was turning gray at the temples, and he had a goatee that was a mixture of brown and gray, mostly gray. He was a shorter man, only about five foot eight or so.

"Mr. Kincannon, please come this way to my office."

I nodded, and he led the way. As we walked along, I noticed that the lab was full of bizarre contraptions. He explained that they were the carcasses of failed projects.

"What kind of failed projects are they?" I asked.

"All in good time, sir. All in good time."

The walls were gray, and cobwebs hung everywhere. There were no windows to the outside, and the floor was bare concrete. I noticed that the air in his place had a weird and unknown smell about it. The whole place was a bit creepy, and creepy is right up my alley. When we walked into his office, I saw he had cobwebs there too, and I chuckled, thinking of my own.

"Please sit down, won't you, Mr. Kincannon? Is something amusing?"

"Sorry, sir. Not at all."

"Very well, Mr. Kincannon …"

"Please call me Jake."

"As you wish, Jake. What I am about to tell you will seem most extraordinary and perhaps even unbelievable, but I assure you it is all fact, which I can and will prove to your utmost satisfaction. But first I have a document for you to sign." He looked around, on, and through his desk franticly. "Wherever did I put that paper?" he said under his breath as he began to shuffle through the books and papers on top of his desk.

I had to hold back from laughing; it was such a comical sight.

"Oh, there it is. You may read it. It is simply an agreement that everything you see or hear or that we discuss will not be disclosed to another person or entity and that you will not write down or record any of the information gleaned here today or from any subsequent meetings, should they occur."

I read through the document and wondered if this was some great government experiment. The paper seemed harmless enough, so I reached for my pen and agreed to it by placing my signature where indicated. I knew there was no getting to first base without it.

"Okay. There you are, Doctor. Now what's so secretive that you wish to show me? Does this have anything to do with the government?"

"Oh heavens, no. This is my work and my work alone."

"Well, you certainly have my curiosity piqued. Can you now explain?"

"Yes, quite right. You see, Jake, I am a scientist and an inventor. I have been working on this project exclusively since my lovely wife, Sheila, was killed. Actually, she died quite violently. She was kidnapped, raped, and murdered as she was on her way home from her job at the Pentagon."

He pushed his wire-rimmed glasses up on his head and quickly pulled a handkerchief from his lab coat pocket and pretended to blow his nose, but his fingers pushed the cloth up to his eyes to absorb the tears that damn near spilled over as he spoke of his wife. I was touched as I imagined being him, with Julie as the victim. I understood his grief.

He returned his handkerchief to his pocket and said, "The police said she was kidnapped as she walked from the building to her car in the parking lot. A man on duty that night, a soldier to be more precise, remembered seeing a black panel truck stop near her as she exited the building. A man jumped out, grabbed her, and pushed her into his vehicle, which then sped out of the parking lot with her and her captor, or captors, inside. They found her naked body in the Potomac the next morning." He paused again and became misty-eyed once more.

"I'm so sorry for your loss, Doc."

"Thank you," he said as he pulled the handkerchief out of his pocket again, wiped his eyes, and blew his nose. Then he cleared his throat and continued, "No one was ever caught. No panel truck was ever found. It was forty-three years ago last month. Somewhere between midnight and 2:00 a.m. on May 11, 1937, to be exact. After my father died a month later, I quit my job with George Washington University and moved directly into his home here in Chicago. When I discovered the entire floor of this building was empty, I had it renovated so I could live and work here. I have a small apartment on the other side of this office. I couldn't bring myself to sell the old house, so I rented it and moved in here. These last forty plus years,

I have worked exclusively on this project, and I did all this for her. I have worked through failure after failure to finally get to this point, and now that I have successfully completed my work, I need your help. Can't you see, Jake? I must have her back."

"But I thought you just said she was … dead?"

"She is, but with your help, I am going to bring her back."

"Now wait, Doc. Are you trying to tell me you can bring the dead back to life?"

"No, not exactly."

I stopped any further talk about raising the dead by standing and preparing to leave. I wasn't sure what this weirdo was all about, but I had heard all I wanted to hear.

"Now wait, Jake. Hear me out, please." He reached into his desk drawer and retrieved an envelope with a bunch of hundred-dollar bills sticking out of it. He slid it across his desk toward me. I quickly sat back down.

"Thank you. Now, as I was saying, I did this for my wife. I miss her terribly, and I have labored long and hard to achieve my goal. I have lived here, eaten here, worked here, and have rarely left this place just for this very reason, just to get to where I am now."

"But how can you afford to do all this without working?"

"My father left me this building we're standing in as well as his house, which, as I said, I have rented out. The money I inherited from my father was a sizable sum. Plus, the rent from the house and this building is enough to last a lifetime, maybe two. My father made his fortune in oil and real estate. Although he lost a considerable amount in the crash of 1929, he was diversified enough to leave me quite well off. In fact, the building we're in is debt free, as is the house, and just the rent from both is enough by itself to sustain my work and me. You can see I live modestly, although my supplies are very expensive. A price I'm more than willing to pay."

I nodded as if to acknowledge that I understood. We had one thing in common; we both owned the houses we grew up in. Then I asked the big question—the question that would show me whether he was a kook, a charlatan, or a genius.

"How are you going to get your dead wife back?"

"Yes, Jake, I understand this all sounds a bit strange, and you may be doubting my sanity at this point. However, I assure you I am quite sane. Now, I did not invent a machine to resurrect the dead, but rather a machine I call a Teleporter."

"What is that?"

"It's a machine that can transport a person or thing backward or forward in time …"

"Are you telling me you invented some sort of time machine?" Now I was really intrigued. This was right up my alley. That plus the money in the envelope kept me glued to my seat.

"Yes, my goal to build this machine was twofold. First and foremost was to go back in time and prevent my wife from being in that parking lot on that fateful day, and a distant second after that was to go back and prevent other crimes of the past that caused great suffering to others, just as the death of my wife did to me. I would even be able to travel forward in time and perhaps warn folks of pending disasters."

"But shouldn't one be very careful because of the possibility of unintended consequences?"

He looked at me strangely and said with a surprised tone in his voice, "Excellent, Jake, excellent! You are absolutely correct, and that is why I must be very careful to study the significance of the individuals. Study their lineage to be sure that the deed was not more than compensated for by some of their offspring."

"Look, Dr. Wells, I don't have difficulty understanding your theoretical proposition, and I appreciate all you're saying, but with all due respect, I just can't accept this without some solid facts. My experience is that most of the cases I take on involving the paranormal, the unexplained, and the fantastic turn out to be hoaxes. Furthermore, to bring your wife back to you now … Well … I mean you're no spring chicken, if you'll pardon me for saying so."

He looked at me for a second and then began to laugh. He laughed so hard I feared he would have a stroke. He once again pushed his glasses up onto his forehead and wiped the tears from his eyes with his handkerchief. This time, he was actually tearing up from laughter.

"No, Jake, I don't wish to bring her forward in time. I want you to do whatever you must to stop her from dying. If you do that, she will come home that fateful night, and we will, as the stories tell us, live happily ever after. In other words, I will have spent the last forty-three years with her."

He continued to laugh through his words, but now it was clear as to why I was there.

"Oh no, I am not—"

He held up his hand and cut me off in midsentence. "Wait, I understand that you find this more than a little hard to believe, so just let me prove it to you so we can move on. I have prepared a little demonstration just for you. Okay?"

"Oh yes, indeed. I insist. Please show me this wonder."

"Very well then. If you'll please come this way."

We walked out another door to his office. There was actually a door in each wall of his office. One had brought us in from the elevator side of the building. This one led to his Teleporter thingie, past even more relics, all of which, he explained, were again more failed attempts at building his time machine. The third door, which he had pointed to earlier when he said he lived there, led to his apartment, and the final was a restroom. I could see it because the door was partially ajar. Because this place was a basement, it had no windows. The overhead fluorescent lighting was strange. Along with the dust-covered, discarded relics of his failures, it was also a bit spooky. And because Doc reminded me somewhat of Dr. Frankenstein, it seemed like the secret place where he had built his monster. He was, in my mind at that point, just some mad scientist who had, like Frankenstein, driven himself mad with his obsession. I was certain that no such fantastic machine could possibly exist. However, if he wanted to pay me to humor him … Well, I wasn't exactly busy, was I?

We went through a passageway and through a locked door. In this room, this very clean and sterile room, which was certainly unlike the rest of the place, was a large, dark gray, almost black, cylindrical machine with two electrode-like things on top. There was a door in the front of this device with a big wheel in the center of it that looked exactly like the watertight hatches of a submarine. In the door, above the wheel, was a large, thick, glass portal. When he spun the wheel to the left, the door eased open and then slid to the right, allowing full accessibility into the thing—this transporter, as he called it. Inside was a raised floor with a hole in it; a large, round grate covered the hole. Tubes ran vertically all around the sidewalls, and another grate-type covered hole like the one on the floor was located directly above it in the ceiling. On the exterior of the machine and to the right of the door was a large panel with many square buttons and lights on it.

"All right, Jake. Watch closely."

The doctor grabbed a large, red-handled lever located to the right of the panel, labeled *power source,* and lifted it straight up. It made a loud click as it locked into place, and the machine began to make a sound similar to a refrigerator when the compressor kicks on, only louder. The panel began to flicker, and numbers began to spin like some kind of large, wall-mounted analog speedometer. Doc explained that the machine was warming up. Soon the noise quieted slightly, and the numbers stopped rolling. From inside the pod, as he sometimes referred to the Teleporter, an eerie green glow pulsated on and off, yet there was no sound, save a very slight hum, as slight as the hum of a neon light. The numbers on the panel seemed to indicate numeric dates and times.

"Now, Jake, pay close attention. The number on the top of the panel is the date, followed by the time, and to the right of that are the coordinates indicating the destination. The next date down is always the actual current date and time, and the coordinates are the location of the Teleporter, or what might be referred to as the beam-out point or ground zero. As you can see, they presently read all zeroes. That is where the machine sits, and this would always be ground zero. So the beam-out point and the return beam-in point are always where the machine is located, or ground zero. You will be sent forward or backward in time from inside the pod, and you will return to the same location, inside the pod."

"Doc, I'm not going anywhere in that … that thing."

"Yes, Jake, quite right. Let's just say for now, theoretical you. Now, the next series of numbers down indicates the date and time for which we preprogram the return, as well as the retrieval beam-out point coordinates. The destination point and the retrieval point are always the exact same coordinates. Again, you can see that they are currently set to ground zero. The fourth series is the date, time, and coordinates for an intermediate stop before the return back to ground zero. This is a critical coordinate. It will be programmed for your office. When successful the Teleporter won't exist, so this coordinate will be set for your trip, and you will arrive back in your office. If you are unsuccessful, the machine will default and bring you back to ground zero. Finally, the fifth and final series is the return to the present date. That date changes each day to the current date to prevent the last travel period from taking a passenger somewhere he or she cannot return from. So let's set the machine to a date in the future, let's say June 12, 2000. We will set the return time for today's date but ten minutes later, and then we will zero out the fourth, or intermediate, coordinates and date."

After Wells programmed the machine to go to the future, I wondered how he would prove it to me. Then he picked up a tripod with a camera on top. The camera had a small device attached to it that he said would take several photos when it arrived in a time-sequenced pattern. Then he set the destination point as the sidewalk outside the building, against the wall. The return point was the inside of the machine at ground zero. There were also security cameras mounted outside the building to cover the area around the ground-floor main entrance.

On the wall to the left of where the pod sat was a bank of monitors where I could see all activity outside the building's entrance and perimeter. After he had everything to his liking, Wells sealed the door and pushed a large red button on the panel. The machine started to whine like a jet engine—slow and relatively quiet at first and then slowly building in speed and sound level. As it seemed to reach the right speed, the vertical tubes inside the pod began to give off a reddish glow, and then the tripod was gone right before my very eyes!

Then the machine began to wind down to an idle. Doc said the machine would continue to idle for trips of an hour or less in duration. On longer trips, the machine would shut itself off, and the clocks would start it ten minutes before beam-in time. The square, gunmetal gray clock on the panel began counting down the seconds and then the minutes. While we waited the ten minutes for the camera to be transported back inside the pod, he said, "Now, Jake, this machine has a great safety feature. If the landing point or beam-in point and date one selected had a physical structure at that exact point that perhaps wasn't there in a different time or was now underwater, the pod would flash a few times, not transport the object forward, and slow back to an idle. Thus, when a human traveled, he or she would not materialize in solid rock or underwater."

"Well, Doc, that's certainly good to know, and I'll keep that in mind."

My kooky friend must have picked up my sarcasm. He furrowed his brow and said, "Humm … quite right."

It all seemed so utterly impossible and unbelievable. The Teleporter began to whine, and I checked my watch, but only five minutes had elapsed. I looked at Doc with what must have been a surprised expression, and he began to chuckle. The dates flashed a couple of times, and the machine's whining became louder again. The same things that had happened the first time happened again, and then the tripod reappeared. After the machine quieted, a green light on the panel came on, and the doctor told me it was now okay to open the hatch, which he did.

"Okay, Doc, what gives? You said you sent it ten minutes into the future. It's only been five."

He began to chuckle again. "I compressed the time by 50 percent. However, I can compress up to as much as one day per year."

"Why?"

"Let's say I wanted to send you back in time with your duration back then being a month, but I didn't want to wait for a full month to get you back. Because we know time can be warped, I created that feature within the machine. Frankly, that was the hardest part. So I send you back, you live a month there, and I bring you back in let's say twenty-four hours. Now back in the past, you have aged a month, but when you return, you have only aged one day. Make sense?"

"Hell no, it doesn't make sense. None of this makes any sense at all! In fact, I'm getting out of here!"

"Now hold on, Jake. Just wait a minute. See the pictures after they are developed, and if you still wish to go, you may—and with the five hundred dollars I promised."

I nodded my agreement, but it was only for the money.

He removed the camera and told me to accompany him to the darkroom so he could develop the pictures. There were ten pictures, one taken each minute, plus one when the camera first landed. He wanted me in the darkroom as they developed so I would not think he had made this all up with some sleight-of-hand parlor trick.

I watched the images slowly begin to appear on the paper. I saw things I had never seen before. The wide-angle lens showed cars like I had never dreamed of and people walking in clothes like I had never seen. Not a single man wore a hat, save a few young people wearing baseball type caps, but they all wore them backward. The women wore very short skirts similar to but not quite as short as the miniskirts that came about in the sixties and were still being worn to some degree in my time. "Wow!" was all I could say.

After the photos dried, we went back to his office, and I studied them more closely, looking for the fake. They looked real enough, and the buildings across the street were the same buildings, but everything else was different. I was dumbfounded. There was even a billboard that read, *We survived Y2K. Buy your new Micro ...* A passing truck blocked the rest of the sign. I wondered, *What the hell is a Y2K?* Yet I still couldn't ... I mean, come on. Time travel? A Teleporter, time machine to the past? Even to the future! I saw it happen, but it was still too much to believe. It had to be a parlor trick, some sleight of hand too quick even for me.

He walked me over to the monitor panel and pulled the film on camera six, which was focused on the front of the building. He ran it back to the time just before the tripod was sent into the future. It was clearly not there, and then it was. Then he fast-forwarded the film exactly nine and a half minutes. The tripod was still there, and as the last thirty seconds ticked away, we watched, and it was gone just before it reappeared inside the pod five minutes from when he sent it. "Wow." Again, I was dumbfounded and speechless.

Doc kept explaining, and we talked for three more hours until he finally convinced me of its legitimacy. Unless he was the best damn magician I had ever seen, my gut, which was almost always reliable, said that this was real. Once I admitted that I believed, he put his hand on my shoulder and said, "Jake, here is my plan. You will travel back in time before my wife's murder, and you will prevent it some way, somehow. And when you are successful, I will know instantly, as she will be with me the second that history is changed ... perhaps."

Then the reality set back in again. "Wait! Hold on, Doc. You want *me* to get into that ... that thing and spew my atoms through time and space? You must be crazy! Why don't you go?"

"I must run the machine, and you are the former homicide detective, not me. Since you deal with the difficult to believe, and that is your specialty, you are the perfect candidate. I would not know how to find and prevent her death, but that is your area of expertise. You have never been married and therefore have no children. You had an excellent record as a homicide detective with our local PD. Now as a PI, your record for earning a living … Well, let's just say it has been less than stellar. You barely eke out enough to pay your secretary, Miss Carson, who I happen to know you have more than a fondness for. I also know that you have tried to keep your engagement secret from your clientele. Yes, you are my man all right, and I am prepared to pay you handsomely for your effort. This could also allow you to solve other crimes of the past after I have researched their role in and effect on the future. This would be the big case you have been waiting for, and it could be followed by many more cases. Why, after my case alone, you would have enough money where you might be able to marry the lovely Miss Julie. Yes?"

"Yeah, yeah … Oh and by the way, what did you mean by 'perhaps'?"

"Excuse me?"

"You said you would know instantly if I was successful *perhaps.*"

"Oh yes, I remember. I simply meant that she would be with me instantly in 1980 perhaps, unless she was to die again after your rescue of her. Don't be alarmed. That's all I meant by what I said. We might then have to rescue again, should that occur."

"Good day, Doctor. I'll show myself out." I snatched up the five hundred dollars from the envelope. "This will cover my time for today as you agreed. Thank you."

"Please give me your decision as soon as possible. Please."

"Sure, Doc. You bet." What part of no didn't he understand?

He escorted me to the elevator, and before he pushed the call button, I stopped him. "One more question, Doc. What's your interpretation of handsomely?"

"Oh, quite right. I was thinking fifty thousand when you accept my proposition … and another fifty thousand upon your completion."

I stood there speechless as he pushed the call button. "Good day, Jake."

"Yeah, yeah." I was dumbfounded … again. I stepped into the elevator and was whisked to the lobby and made my way to the street.

CHAPTER 7

CONTEMPLATION

As I walked back toward my building, I stopped in the Grub Pub, a bar and grill on the ground floor of the building next to mine, for a sandwich and a drink. This had been a favorite eatery of mine when I was on the force, so when I had found office space next door to it, I was quite happy. I had eaten there damn near every day, and now Julie and I had lunch there most days.

It was now well past lunchtime, and I was famished. Plus, I needed a good stiff drink after all the stuff the good doctor had packed my ears with. I walked through the door, and it looked the same as it always did: the dim light, old Fred behind the bar, Dolly waiting tables. Sitting at the bar were the usual folks that congregated to drink. This place attracted the high brows and the low brows. It was one of those places. People would say, "Have you ever eaten at the Grub Pub?" and then look at you strangely if you said no. The patrons sat and drank and talked of glories long since passed, wasting their precious time away. A few businessmen were also having a late lunch. Cigarette smoke hung in the air, and the smell of food emanated from the back.

Everything was the same. Everyone was the same. Except for me. How could I be the same after what I had just heard and witnessed? No, I would never be the same again. It was as though someone had opened the proverbial Pandora's box. There was no way back to my ignorant bliss of this morning. No way to put the genie back into the bottle.

I pulled up a barstool. "Hey, Fred. Give me a double Daniels on the rocks."

"Okay, Mac. Comin' right up."

While he knew my name—in fact, he knew the names of most of his regulars—he still called everyone Mac. Good ol' Fred.

"Hey, doll. What's good in the kitchen?" I asked as I grabbed Dolly around the waist and gave her a big kiss on the cheek.

"Get your mitts off me, ya big galoot." Dolly smiled. "I got some good pot roast or one of those Reubens you like so much."

"Good. Give me the Reuben, doll face."

"Oh, you!" she said as I gave her a love pat on the rump as she walked away.

Dolly was a great gal, probably in her late fifties, with bleached-blonde hair and a great figure for her age. I bet she had been a real looker in her day, but too much sun and too much fun had taken its toll on her skin, and her false teeth clicked a little when she talked. But she was a real sweetheart, and she had stuck by ol' Fred all these years, and he still refused to marry her. What a pair they were. They reminded me a little of Matt Dillon and Miss Kitty in the old TV series in that regard. Kitty was Matt's girl, but he wouldn't marry her. By now you've probably realized that I'm a big movie, TV fan.

"Here's your double D, Mac."

"Thanks, pal."

Ol' Fred, he looked like a hundred, but he was also built like a bull. He was hunched over with his shoulders rounded in, but nobody messed with him. The arms on that man looked like those of a weight lifter, and he had a tattoo on his left bicep of a bulldog's face that said *Devil Dog* under it. He had a tattoo of an eagle, globe, and anchor on his right bicep. He always wore a white, short-sleeve T-shirt and a white apron. He rolled up the sleeves of his shirt so everyone could see both entire tattoos, and he kept a pack of smokes rolled up in the left sleeve, just like he had done as a teenager. He still wore his now gray hair short, in a flat top, but the bald spot on top kept getting bigger.

Nobody had to guess what branch of the service he had been with. His voice was like a bear growling, it was so deep. I always thought that was another part of the intimidation factor. I wondered what ol' Fred would say if I told him what I had just experienced. He'd probably send for the men in the white suits. I took a big pull from my drink and exhaled like the weight of the world had been lifted off my shoulders. Two more pulls, and my drink was gone and the Reuben arrived.

"Hey, Fred. Give me a tall, cold draft."

"On its way, Mac," came the growl from the far end of the bar.

I ate and slowly sipped my beer and killed a good hour there. At about 1600, I paid the tab and walked back to my office. When I walked through the door, Julie was tidying up my desk—a never-ending job.

I sat down with a thud. "Please have a seat, darling. If you learned something that was so unbelievable, so incredible, and it offered you a chance to take a very dangerous but also a very exciting adventure, what would you do?"

"Well, I … I …" She paused and got this sort of dreamy-eyed expression. She stared out the window and then resumed. "I would go, and I would live it to the max and try to make it last as long as it could." She continued to stare out the window as though whatever she was thinking was playing out right before her eyes.

"Julie … Julie?" I had to snap my fingers twice.

"Huh? Oh sorry, Jake."

I thought it cute how she always called me Jake at the office, Mr. Kincannon in front of clients, and lots of endearments when we were anywhere alone outside the office.

"Thought you left me for a moment."

"Oh, I'm sorry. I guess I did sail away for a moment. What you said made me think of my goal to someday visit Hawaii and sail back and forth between the islands. Though sometimes I think it will never happen." She hung her head and seemed to get a little blue.

I felt bad, so I walked over and hugged her to comfort her. I dropped the subject, and we decided to go home. I would share the details of my time away from the office with her only if I was even remotely considering it.

The next week was a weird one! I learned things I almost wished I hadn't. Doc's crazy plan began to make more and more sense to me, and that had me questioning my sanity. Traveling through time in his crazy Teleporter machine … why, I could die in that confounded contraption. Or be dumped in some other lifetime, never to be seen or heard from again.

However, every time I convinced myself it was a crazy idea, I would start thinking about it some more and begin to argue with myself. It was like I was some sort of glutton for punishment, or was it the money and what it could do for Julie and me? Each day, I anxiously checked with Julie for any job that would take my mind off Doc and his machine. It had been a week now, and I decided that if there was no new job today, I was going to see Doc.

"Julie, do I have any appointments today?"

"Just your buddy Tom for lunch."

"Be a doll and call him and cancel for me, the usual something came up bit."

I walked, or should I say paced, in my office for two hours and drank three more cups of coffee, just hoping the phone would ring with a case, but when I did finally get a call, it was Doc wondering if I had come to a decision. I told him I would come over to discuss his crazy idea in more detail.

"Julie, I'm going back to Dr. Wells's office."

"Sure, Jake. When will you be back?"

"Couple hours, I guess."

I hurried down to Doc's office before I changed my mind. Then I took the strange elevator ride to the basement level, although this time the operator didn't ask me my name. Guess I must have been important. When the doors opened, there Doc stood waiting with a big grin on his mug.

"Doc, are you absolutely sure this machine of yours will do everything you say it will?"

"Well, hello to you too, and yes, I am positive. I'd bet my life on it."

I laughed sarcastically. "No, you're betting *my* life on it!"

"Yes, quite right. I see your point, and yes, I'd bet your life on it too."

"Okay, Doc. I changed my mind. I'll do it. I must be out of my mind, though. But it's going to cost you large, like one hundred thousand dollars—*up front*, in cash—delivered to me before my departure. When I have it, two mornings later I will climb in your contraption."

"But—"

"No buts. Take it or leave it, and frankly I hope you leave it."

The next person to speak would lose. He looked at me as if to gauge my seriousness. Then he slowly began to chuckle and patted me on the back, saying, "Good lad. Very good! I agree to all your terms."

"Okay, Doc. Now you're talkin' my language."

"Now that you're on board, please don't call me Wilson. You can call me Will or Doc or anything, but not Wilson. Never did like that name."

"Okay, Doc. Whatever you say," I said with a slight chuckle. "Although, I never have called you Wilson."

"Huh? Oh yeah, quite right … and see that you don't!"

"Doc, there are a few things troubling me about this trip, and I'm surprised I didn't think of it until last night. I saw the camera and tripod go through and return unscathed, but how do we know that something living can make the trip and not come back … well, DOA?"

Doc laughed. "Do you think I didn't think of that and test it to be sure it was safe before I called you?"

"Doc, as I'm sure you can understand, I need to be as sure as you are about this."

"I understand. I'll be right back."

Doc walked into the next room and a few minutes later returned carrying a monkey.

"What's with the monkey, Doc?"

"This is Lulu, and she's not a monkey. She's a forty-pound orangutan, a member of the ape family. Lulu, say hello to Jake."

With that, Lulu held out her long arm as if to shake hands with me and curled up her upper lip. Doc informed me that was her way of smiling. I took her hand and shook it gently.

"Watch Lulu here. She's made the trip several times."

Doc took her to the machine and sat her on the screen. Then he fired up the controls and sent her to somewhere and in a few seconds brought her back. Granted, she wasn't gone but a moment, but she disappeared from the pod and then reappeared.

"Okay, what is your other concern?"

"I need to know if I'm thinking straight on this time travel stuff. If I go back and save her, that changes history, so what need would there be for you to build this machine and rescue me?"

"Quite right and an excellent query, and here is the very simple answer. When you materialize, you will be in the pod, but the pod will likely be in a different location. I will have no memory of anything that happened at the moment Sheila doesn't die. But Sheila will remember everything. I mean she will know that you saved her life, and you must tell her about my machine, and you will instruct her that she *must* have me retrieve one of the two dark green, padlocked footlockers. They will be identical in their content. I made two in case something unanticipated should happen to one of them. One is already sealed under the staircase to the basement of my home that my father left to me in his will. It will have no access; therefore, it will have to be torn open to retrieve the footlocker. The second footlocker has already been sealed here in the false wall beside the bathroom. Come with me." He led me there and pointed out the wall. "It's inside that wall. As you can see, that wall is newer than any of the rest of the walls, as it was finished the day before I called you."

"Yeah okay, two hidden trunks. How does that answer my question?"

"Jake, your youth increases your lack of patience. In these trunks are all the plans and specs to build the Teleporter you see before you, without, however, all the trials and errors that I went through. It will also tell me where to buy the materials now readily available that were so hard for me to locate in the early years. I will be able to build an identical unit in less than thirty days and bring you back home to your time."

"What about the coordinates?"

"They are there as well. Jake, stop worrying. I've been over this a thousand times. I got it all."

"Doc, is there anything I should have asked you that I didn't?"

He thought for a moment and then said, "Yes. Yes, there is. You didn't ask me what happens to you if I drop dead before you return."

"Oh yeah. What about that?"

Doc was really yucking it up now, and when he finally stopped, he reminded me that the settings were automatic, "Once set, it would run completely on its own, even in the event of a complete power blackout, until history changed. However, once changed, the machine will never have been built, and Sheila must tell me of the footlockers. See? Very simple. Here's what you must not forget. You must be back on the beam point at the exact time the machine fires, or you will, as they say, miss the boat."

"Doc, you mean if I miss the time, I'm stranded in that time forever?"

"No, Jake. The machine is set to try again four more times, once every three hours. After that, you are there for the duration."

"Doc, I want you to promise that after the four automatic recoveries are complete, if you haven't recovered me, you will try twice a day, every day at noon and midnight, until I'm recovered."

"Well, yes, we can do that, and I'll make notes to that effect for the record. In my safe deposit box will be my diary with any instructions that may need to be added to the information in the footlocker and instructions as to who will inherit it in case of my untimely demise. My last will and testament will be there as well."

"Hold on … what if something happens to you *after* I'm successful but before you complete the new Teleporter?"

"Since nothing happened to me before, the only variable would be Sheila herself. But if that variable should kill or render me incapable of building a new Teleporter … well then have a good life in the thirties, but the odds are astronomically in your favor."

"Okay, Doc, I'm satisfied that you've covered the bases."

Now I had to get to work. I had to research his wife's murder, what he remembered and what the papers had reported. I soon learned that everything was as Doc had said about her death; it was a terrible tragedy and one that I would have to prevent. I told Julie of my plans and told her to pull our ads. We discussed the pros and cons of this venture until she finally agreed, though reluctantly. I was going to be in the employ of Dr. Wilson Wells to find the murderer of his wife and try to prevent her death.

Two weeks went by, and I was now well versed on all that had happened on that date. My assignment was to travel back in time to arrive on the morning of May 7, 1937, and depart at exactly midnight on May 10, 1937. I was supposed to meet up with Doc and Sheila and work it out to pick her up from work that fateful day or see that she wouldn't be there that day.

Doc had prepared a file for me to present to himself, a much younger himself, on my arrival. This file was so packed with information that Doc felt his younger self would believe the crazy story I would tell him. It even contained newspaper clippings from his future about him, the murder of his wife, and a write-up of a baseball game that would be played in Washington two days after I arrived in the past. The game would be between the Washington Senators and the Cleveland Indians.

At this earlier stage of the doc's life, he was a professor at a local college in the Washington, DC, area. There would be additional information in that file that no one but him could possibly know. That additional information was of such a personal nature that I was not privy to it. The overwhelming amount of information contained in this file would be enough to convince him of its accuracy and authenticity, and my travel through time.

My plan for something going wrong was also planned out during this period. The money Doc was to give me prior to my flight would be deposited in my corporate account, which Julie was a signatory. I prepared a will leaving all my worldly positions to Julie Carson, she was given a copy, and we added her to the deed to my house. My attorney would deliver the will upon my disappearance, as prescribed by law. Julie knew she was to use the money as she saw fit, live in the house and use whatever of my things she desired, until the will could be probated. If I returned, no problem; Julie and I would live on as planned, only richer.

CHAPTER 8

THE NIGHT BEFORE

Tomorrow was the big day, a day that would start an adventure that would end up with me as a hero or a corpse. It might also leave me a hero stuck in another time to live out my remaining days. However, after working with Doc the past few weeks, I had come to trust him and actually enjoy his company. I was much more convinced that his machine would do what he said it would do.

Since today was the eve of my great adventure, Julie and I decided to go out for dinner. We went to Anthony's Bistro, two blocks from the office. It was my favorite restaurant; it was small and usually quiet with an intimate atmosphere, not to mention good food and service.

When we arrived, Anthony greeted us and took us to a very nice table overlooking the Chicago River in an especially quiet corner. Did you know the Chicago River is the only river in the world that flows backward? It's true, but I digress. Anthony knew from our earlier conversation when I had made the reservation that tonight was a special night. As we sat there looking out at the lights of the Chicago night reflecting off the river and listened to the soft jazz playing in the background, I wondered if I had just signed my death warrant. I would not even breathe a word of that to Julie. I knew I was convinced one minute that all was fine and then wondered the next if I was setting my own course for destruction. Oh, wait till I tell you what's ahead.

We sipped our drinks and sat at the small dining table with its white linen tablecloth and white cloth napkins twirled into fine crystal water glasses. A small bouquet of flowers sat in the vase at the center of the table. My thoughts were on Julie. In fleeting moments, I would wonder, what if I died and never saw Julie, or anyone else for that matter, again? I wondered if this was what a prisoner felt like as he waited to be led to the electric chair or was stranded with people he didn't know and from whom there was no escape. Lord knew I had seen enough of those situations in my days on the police force.

Her soft voice snapped me back to the present. "Penny for your thoughts?"

"Oh, I was just thinking how much I love you and how beautiful you are."

"Are you sure you're not thinking about tomorrow? Are you having any worries about never seeing me again?"

"Well, maybe thinking a little about tomorrow, but there's no doubt I'll see you again. After all I've learned from Doc about this trip, why it's no more dangerous than simply flying to DC. In fact, I'll be back faster than if I were flying." I thought I stated that with enough confidence and conviction to assure anyone of my safe return. Still, Julie just gave me that look of hers. The look I had come to recognize as meaning *I hear ya, but I ain't buying stock in it.*

"At the house is a large, wooden box. Inside are the keys to my Corvette and my set to the house. Also inside are the bankbooks, both checking and savings, personal and company. There's enough money to cover everything until I return in a less than a week. There's also the contact information for Dr. Wells. I have also updated my will, just in case. You should know that I've left everything I own to you—"

"No, you can't do that!" she interrupted.

"Julie, listen. You know that I have to, and why let what's there simply go to the state? You can use it far more than the crooked politicians can. I couldn't bear for them to get it. Anyway, it's not that much. However, before I leave, I will be giving you a certified check payable to the firm. Please deposit it right away and pay any outstanding debts."

"Oh, *Jake*, do we have to talk about this? It's as though you're already dead. It creeps me out."

"Julie, I love you, and I will return, but one can die crossing the street, so I must know that you can function if a one-in-a-million freak thing should happen. Okay?"

She nodded the affirmative but not convincingly. I finished telling her everything I could think of and topped it with a smart remark: "Besides, if I don't make it back, you get the house, the money, the Vette, everything."

With that, she jumped up from the table and moved smartly in the direction of the ladies' room. After she left, the waiter returned. "Are you folks ready to order?"

I sent him away until Julie returned with her composure back and acting kind of playfully. The waiter returned with his same query, and Julie quickly jumped in. "Gee, I believe we are ready. How about you, *Jake?*"

I smiled and nodded my agreement.

"I think I'll have the chicken cordon bleu and a garden salad with blue cheese dressing. May I order for you, *Jake?*" Julie said with surprising calmness.

I simply nodded and smiled. At least I think I did.

"And for him, a T-bone steak, rare, with a baked potato, no butter but extra sour cream, and a garden salad with blue cheese dressing."

"Very well, ma'am. Excellent choices," the waiter replied as he gathered the menus and then departed.

We talked about a sundry of things, and soon the waiter returned with our salads. I thanked him, and we picked up where we left off without missing a beat. Before we knew it, the waiter was back with the main course.

"Oh, you haven't had time to eat your salads. Shall I take these back to the kitchen?"

Julie smiled and said, "Oh no. Just set them down. We'll manage. We've been talking way too much."

"Yes, just leave them." I wanted to say something to him or else he might have thought I was mute.

"Very well then."

"Let's eat, shall we?" I said, trying to regain some stature in the conversation.

That night, I saw a side of Julie that I had never seen before, and I liked it. I liked it a lot. She had courage, and it was beginning to show. I knew how she felt because I felt the same way, and frankly, had she pushed a little harder, I might have aborted the whole mission. But she bucked up, and that helped bolster me as well.

We made more small talk while we ate, and giggled a bit like school kids. And when dinner was over, we continued to talk about all manners of things over a liqueur for her and a brandy for me. I noticed we both seemed to avoid conversation that had anything to do with long-term activities.

So, after we had sat long enough to numb at least my butt, I walked her to the street, and we decided to walk along the river for a while. The night air along the river was chilly, so I wrapped my arm around her. When I did that, she stopped and looked into my eyes. That was the sign I had been waiting for. I allowed no time for a change of heart, and I kissed her. And oh what a kiss it was.

It was far from our first kiss, but in a strange way it sort of seemed to me like it was. Her lips were familiar and as soft as a butterfly's wing and as succulent as a ripe piece of cantaloupe. Her skin smelled of magnolias and honeysuckle, and her eyes staring up at me looked like little pools of the bluest ocean at calm. Every nerve in my body was on fire. If I died at that exact moment, the mortician would not have been able to remove my smile of utter contentment.

We eventually arrived home, and we wasted no time enjoying what I hoped would last a lifetime. But the future was vastly unknown.

CHAPTER 9

BACK IN TIME

On the big day, I awoke very early and unassisted. That was unusual for me, as normally the alarm was banging like crazy before I even stirred. I knew what was scheduled to happen today, and I was extremely nervous. I had never been this way in combat or on my job as a homicide detective, even when we were involved in shootouts. But I was committed to doing this thing, at least until I thought of Julie. That caused me to want to call Doc and say the gig was off.

I pushed myself to the bathroom to shower and shave. I pondered my face in the mirror and wondered what a beautiful girl like Julie saw in a grizzled ex-jarhead, ex-cop, and now PI who didn't have enough work to keep it going and was just waiting for a break, *this* break. That last thought brought me full circle and back to the well-paying gig for Doc.

Okay. Scrape the whiskers off the old mug and hit the shower. In an hour, I was ready to leave and had had some breakfast and coffee. The house was quiet, and Julie was still asleep, I thought, as she hadn't come bounding through the door like she usually did when she was up. Yes, she still had her own room. She refused to give it up until after we were married. We just ran back and forth.

I checked things out, took my bag to the foyer, and called a cab. I turned, and there she was at the top of the steps, so I went quickly to her. She was misty-eyed, and I held her until she pulled it together. She then attempted to put on the stiff upper lip, but its trembling gave away her true feelings about this trip. I did my best to convince her until the cab blew his horn. We gave each other one last long kiss to tide me over until my return, which I assured her would be in just a few days of her time.

Twenty minutes later, I was taking the terrace ride in the elevator. Doc's expression when he opened the door and saw me standing there was one of relief.

"What's the matter, Doc? Did you think I wouldn't show?"

"I must admit, I was a bit worried. Jake, are you ready, and do you thoroughly know your mission?"

"Yes, Doc, I do. And in a few hours, your wife shall be at your side, and you'll have over four decades of memories that were stolen from you. You just make sure you get me home alive and in one piece and with all the pieces in their rightful places."

"No problem. You just get back to the beam point *before* 2:00 a.m. I will set the machine to retrieve at midnight, the safest time because we don't know her exact time of death. Then every fifteen minutes and finally at 1:55. If you are still there at the time of her original death, you will be stranded there, at least until I build a new Teleporter."

"Thanks for the heads-up, but I plan to be on the midnight express home. Hey wait, it will be midnight there, which will be my here because I'll be there in Washington, DC, in 1937, but what time will it be here in Chicago in 1980?"

We both laughed. If you think that was confusing, how'd ya like to be me?

When we both stopped laughing, Doc said, "I have warped the time so you will be gone two days by our time. Why, you'll be home in time for a late dinner, provided you are teleported before she doesn't die—don't forget that."

"Are you kidding!"

"Oh, Jake, I almost forgot. Come with me."

Doc walked me over to a closet where he had me change into period-style clothes. Then he handed me a period-style suitcase filled with similar style clothes and instructed me to take my personal effects from my suitcase and stow them in this suitcase. But I was to take nothing that did not exist in that time. He then handed me a round tube about two inches in diameter and about a foot long.

"What's this for?" I asked.

"If you need to contact me for any reason, have a question, need anything, or need to send something to me, put it in the tube and place it on the beam site at midnight or noon and then wait. I will send the tube right back, either with the item or answer you need immediately or with a note that will tell you that I have to acquire the item or info and will send it the next midnight in another tube. This is our only means of communication while you are away. Do you understand?"

"Got it, Doc. Well, I'll see you on the flip."

"One more thing. This morning I sent a locked trunk to my home that I have rented out to be put in the attic in a locked room. I will then find it for future use."

I thought I understood. If time changed, he wouldn't be living in this basement. He would most likely be living with Sheila in the house that had such sentimental value to him.

I stuffed the tube and the introduction file into my suitcase with the already packed essentials for the trip. I picked the suitcase up, and stepped into the Teleporter. My heart was pounding with fear. When Doc closed the door and spun the locking handle, I felt my sphincter pucker. This was a feeling of being alone and uncertain. I said a prayer as I heard the whine that meant I was seconds from gone. When the tubes started to glow, I held my breath and closed my eyes. I heard the whining grow to an almost unbearable loudness, and then I felt a short, quick sensation like my stomach coming up into my throat.

Suddenly the noise and the lifting of my stomach stopped, and I opened my eyes to find myself standing in a semicrouched position with my fingers in my ears and a suitcase at my side. People looked at me, and they must have wondered who this weird man was. Being instantly embarrassed, I quickly assumed a normal posture. The smile I feigned must have looked like one of those sick smiles a guy gets when he gets punched in the gut and tries to mask the pain like it didn't hurt.

The last thing I had experienced just prior to opening my eyes was a noise that began as a slight whining sound and became louder and louder until I thought my eardrums would burst. Must have been the reason for my fingers in my ears. It was followed by a sensation of my stomach lifting. It reminded me of that very same feeling I discovered at about age six while riding in the backseat of my father's Hudson, when he would traverse a vertical curve at a high speed.

Having started over from the beginning, now my story catches back up to where I first left off.

My last thought as the noise began and my stomach began to lift, was that it had all been explained. The logical part of my brain said all was A-Okay, but the emotional side of my brain was in sheer horror! Now standing there, however, all I could remember was that one little thought, but what did it mean? My mind was totally blank. If you haven't experienced it, you can't really grasp what it's like to be looking at things and have no memory of anything. It's truly terrifying. There must have been sound, basic facts deep in my brain though, as I somehow knew the people walking around were like me, and I had no innate fear of them. But all the familiar things I knew I should know were gone.

There I stood on the corner of a busy intersection, wondering, *Where am I? Who am I? How did I get here, and why am I here, wherever the heck here is?* Sounds of moving and stopping cars in the intersection, some blowing their horns, didn't seem unfamiliar, but neither did they seem familiar. The folks who had been staring at me had moved on, and now people were just walking by at a hurried pace, chatting with one another. Walls of office buildings and shops in all directions surrounded me, yet nothing seemed familiar. I was in a big city, but it wasn't Chicago. *That's it! I must be from Chicago.* I kept pondering why nothing looked familiar and who I was. Fortunately for me, within seconds, images began to slowly coalesce in my consciousness, some sketchy at first. I remembered a case I was working on. *Oh, I'm a cop ... no, wait. A private eye. It's coming to me.*

The fog in my head slowly began to clear, much too slowly for my liking, and I started to see bits and pieces of things about a case I had been invited to solve. Why this case? Was I here for something to do with that case? But I had solved that case, hadn't I? Was there more to it? More memories began to return. It felt as if my brain was being fed information, and I began to feel light-headed from the rush.

I noticed a coffee shop on the corner across the street, so I waited for the light to change and the traffic to stop to allow me safe passage to the other side. I crossed the street and stared at a maze of automobiles; they were beginning to resemble cars that I knew, but they seemed older than what I remembered. They all seemed newer in condition than my brain seemed to think they should be. Was I dreaming? I pushed open the door to the coffee shop, and as I entered, a little bell over the door rang, giving off its tinkling sound. I looked at the people; they were dressed as people did in earlier times and like the people I had seen outside. Why did I think that? They sat talking and drinking coffee with breakfast or doughnuts. All seemed so normal, but still somehow it looked strange to me.

A stack of newspapers sat next to the cash register at the front of the long, red counter lined with permanently mounted chrome barstools with padded, red vinyl covering. Copies of Norman Rockwell paintings hung on the antique white walls, and the large, plate-glass windows that adorned the front wall and half the long sidewall allowed me to continue to observe the unending procession of antique cars that streamed by. Three huge, black fans that hung from the ceiling gave off a slight whirring sound as they turned slowly. However, something was very wrong. Everything was old, but not like I was in an antique store or on a movie set; it was more like I didn't belong there. I saw things that weren't part of my personal history, and some things predated my memory. Although somehow they also seemed familiar, as though I were watching an old, black-and-white movie. No, it was more like I was in an old movie, but it was in living color.

I sat at the first stool and glanced at the *Washington Times-Herald* newspaper. *Am I in Washington, DC? No wonder things look unfamiliar. But what's with these headlines? They can't be real!* There, covering almost the entire front page, was the story and pictures of the Hindenburg airship disaster as it exploded over Lakehurst, New Jersey. *This is old news. I read about this in school.* Then I looked at the date of the paper. It was May 7, 1937. This had to be some kind of dream. I ordered a cup of coffee and downed it quickly. The caffeine seemed to help some. I began to feel a sense of normality slowly return to my body and brain. The headlines took my mind away from my memory problems and filled it with new questions.

Maybe I need even more caffeine. Perhaps that would help speed my recovery. I asked the young waitress for a refill. She was pretty and very friendly and wore a white dress that was more like a uniform. Her brown hair was done up in an old, slightly familiar hairstyle and covered in a black fishnet-type hairnet; there was a pencil stuck in it as well. The only thing spoiling her appearance was the way she chewed and snapped her chewing gum. I drank the coffee down quickly. I sat there stunned by the possibilities that just didn't seem real.

This was where I began reliving the werewolf case and was interrupted at the point where I was about to die at the killer's hands when the young waitress suddenly interrupted my reliving the horror of that event. This is where the waitress saved me, "Sir, would you care for anything else? Sir?"

When she broke into my remembering that werewolf case with her query, I wasn't happy. Could I pick up where I left off?

"Why, ah, yes, sure, more coffee."

"Yes, sir."

As she poured another refill, a customer approached the cash register, which was to my immediate left.

"Hi, Julie. I'm ready to pay up."

"Just a sec, Bill."

She returned the pot to the burner and turned back to the customer, wiping her hands on her apron and looking at the check she had left with him when he ordered. "Now, let's see what the damages are today. Was everything okay?"

"Yes, ma'am."

Then it hit me. *Julie. Oh my God. Julie!* Julie was the name of my girl too. I took a chug of the coffee she had just served. As I drank more hot coffee, everything else began to flood my brain. Hearing the name Julie caused me to remember my Julie and where I had met her, which caused me to remember that I was indeed a PI and had my own business, which in turn reminded me of Doc. I was thirsty to regain all my memory and getting jittery from all the coffee, so I ordered a sandwich, thinking that maybe food would also help me clear up the remaining mystery.

As I drank and ate, I began to feel even better, and my memory seemed almost fully restored. That gave me a sense of calm that not even all that caffeine could dissuade. I knew exactly who I was, where I was, and how I had gotten there. More importantly, I knew exactly *why* I was there. The last time I had experienced a memory loss like that was when I was a cop and was hit from behind and knocked unconscious by a perp. In that incident, like now, my memory had been gone, but it returned relatively quickly, much more quickly than this time. But I was certain I hadn't been knocked unconscious this time. But then it dawned on me that the reason I was so into that nightmarish recollection as my memory was returning was that the werewolf case was my first major case as a PI.

Now that my memory was intact, here was the riddle: I had just traveled from Chicago, Illinois, to Washington, DC. Not unusual, except

I left Chicago at 0700 and arrived in Washington at 0800. Fast, right? Yes, especially when you consider the one-hour time difference between the two cities. But wait, that's not all. I didn't arrive by plane, train, or automobile. They were all too slow. Here's a clue: I left Chicago in 1980 and arrived in Washington in 1937. That was what I had just remembered, and now you know. Now the missing pieces were complete, and I had filled in all the blank spaces. I remembered everything now. This was just the beginning. I had to get back on my time plan. If I missed the opportunity of time, my reason and risk for being there would fail. The reason for my being there, in an unfamiliar town more than five hundred miles from home, was an attempt to prevent a heinous crime.

"Julie, may I have my check, please?" She handed it to me, and I paid her. "Thank you, Julie. Would you be kind enough to direct me to the nearest hotel?" She gave me the directions, and out I went to the sound of the tinkling bells. I certainly walked out of the diner a different man than walked in. I was 100 percent back to normal. I paused to let my eyes drink in this piece of history. Wow, what a sight. I started to walk in the direction Julie had told me to go. Man, this city was incredible—the buildings, the greenery, and the old cars that looked like they were new. Unbelievable! It dawned on me as people stared at me that they must have thought I was a tourist. It was a good thing Doc had had me change into period clothes, or they would really be noticing me.

I walked into the hotel lobby and secured a room. Then it also dawned on me as I paid the desk clerk that my money was dated later than the year I was in. Fortunately, she didn't notice. She just stuffed the bills into the cash register. Julie had done the same thing. I didn't worry about Julie, as money was going in and out of that cash register at an alarming rate. By now, some other poor slob was walking around with that one-dollar bill. I couldn't concern myself with that; I had important things to accomplish. Doc had messed up on the money thing, and I sure hoped that was his only mistake. If anyone caught one of these newer bills, they'd arrest me for counterfeiting. Then I'd never get home! I'd have to exchange my money with Doc at midnight. Hopefully they were not as suspicious in these times.

It seemed like most of the people were talking about whether we would be at war soon with Germany or not. It was odd to be hearing this, and the people had no clue about Japan. After I checked in, unpacked, and rested awhile, I listened to the radio, missing my TV. I fell asleep, and when I awoke, it was late afternoon. I freshened up and went back out to get some dinner. On my way past the front desk, I asked the lady who was now working there if she'd ever heard of Pearl Harbor.

She looked at me with a puzzled expression and then said, "That's somewhere in the Caribbean, isn't it?"

"Yeah, that's right," I said as I turned away, rolled my eyes, and walked out.

One could have a ball with things like that, and as I walked down the street to a local restaurant, I remembered what Doc had said: *"Don't try to warn people of coming disasters. They will lock you up for being a nutcase, and back then they did lobotomies and electroshock therapy."* I would stay clear of any of that for sure.

I had a really nice dinner, and, wow, was it cheap. These latter years of the Depression were not as bad as history told us. There were a lot of people in soup lines still, but not like I had seen in the old newsreels. But with some money, I could live like a king here in this time.

When I arrived back at the hotel, as I walked by the front desk to my room, I heard, "Mister … Oh hey, mister."

I turned to see if she was talking to me, and she was. The first thing that went through my mind was the money I had paid with for my room, but as I walked over to her, she said, "We were wrong."

"Excuse me?"

"You know you asked me about Pearl Harbor, and I guessed it was in the Caribbean, and you said right? Well, I checked. We were both wrong. It's in Hawaii. It's a US naval base in Hawaii. Just wanted to set you straight. Have a good evening."

"Thank you. Can you imagine what Billy Mitchell would have said?"

"Who?"

I just smiled and wished her a good night as I turned and walked away. Then I turned back. "Oh, by the way, would you give me a shout at say … 2315?"

"What's that, mister?"

"Ah … 11:15."

"No, I mean why do you want me to shout at you?"

I gave a sick laugh as I realized I had to be careful with slang from my time, as it may be misinterpreted, just like this. "Oh, that's an expression from back home. I mean call my room, please. Sorry."

"Oh sure. You must be a military man?"

"Yes, ma'am. Thank you."

I listened to the radio, and as I feared, I dozed off. But I got my 2315 call, and at 2330 I headed out with the tube Doc had given me. I wrote a note to him to send me some money but to make sure that it was all dated for or prior to 1937. Before midnight, I placed the tube exactly where I had been standing when I landed, so to speak, and then stood back. At midnight straight up, it disappeared right in front of my eyes! So, as I was instructed, I waited. In less than five minutes, the tube reappeared. Inside were three twenties, a ten, and a note that said he would have to send more tomorrow night, as that was all he had in older bills. The note also said for me to send the tube back at 1800, and he would send more old money. I was fortunate that the few singles I had on me when I arrived in 1937 were not newer bills from my time in 1980. Now the dates were wrong but so small that they were not as likely to be noticed. However, the much larger lettering denoting Silver Certificate or Reserve Note at the top of the bill would be more likely to be spotted. Reserve Notes didn't exist until 1964. The one-dollar bill prior to 1964 was titled a Silver Certificate and a Reserve Note after 1964.

I took my bounty and returned to my room. As I listened more to the radio, I got a brainstorm. I decided on a slight change of plan. I would *not* hook up with Doc and Sheila, just Sheila. If I understood this time jumping thing, if young Doc knew what I was there for prior to her not dying, assuming I was successful, he would know what the real history did to her. If he was unaware of my reason for being there, and I saved her, he would never know of it. The change would erase the Doc that I knew and that he knew in 1980. If I could save her without involving him, he would have no memory of her brutal killing and thus be spared all that pain. Tomorrow I would track down only Sheila.

CHAPTER 10

JULIE, SHEILA, AND CRYSTAL

I had learned a lot about Sheila and her job at the Pentagon, even her office phone number, from Doc before I left, and I carried what I hoped would be enough information to convince her and/or the young Doc that I was from the future. As Doc said, he would leave the details to me.

My new plan was to get Sheila alone, show her what would happen to her, and have her simply avoid going to work that day. If I could do that, that would involve the least amount of risk of changing the future in some catastrophic manner. Today I would call her at about 0930 hours and invite her to lunch the next day.

I walked to the diner next to my hotel, had some breakfast, and thought about how I would entice a perfect stranger to have lunch with me or meet with me in her office or after work. I ran the plan through my mind as I had my coffee with a couple eggs, bacon, and toast. The food there was great. The eggs were exactly as I ordered them, sunny-side up with the yokes all wet for toast dipping; the bacon was rendered out nice and crisp; and the rye toast was hot and crunchy, not burnt, with just the right amount of real butter. The coffee was so good I kept nodding on the refill as it passed by.

Plus, it was a small place. It made me feel secure to be in a place without large groups of people. It seemed like I fit in okay, as no one seemed to look at me funny. That was a good thing. The last thing I needed was some beat cop asking me questions I would not be able to answer.

I grabbed a paper from the rack and began to read the latest news. When I saw the date, May 8, 1937, it still looked strange to me. The headlines were still about the crash of the Hindenburg, which happened in Lakeside, New Jersey, just the day before I arrived. Funny, I knew the highlights of that disaster from history, but I would have never remembered the date or exactly where it happened. Now chances were I would never forget it or the minor details that never made recorded history.

I hung out until it was time to make my call to Sheila. I returned to my room to phone her. I noticed the phone was heavier than the phones of my day, and I began dialing the number Doc had given me on the old rotary dial. It seemed so slow compared to the push buttons on the phones I was used to dialing. I guessed that was where the term *dialing* had come from. We still call it that in my day, though it would be more accurate to say "pushing the number." But wouldn't that have sounded strange to say.

The receptionist answered quickly.

"May I please speak with Sheila Wells?"

"One moment, sir."

"Mrs. Wells. May I help you?"

"Mrs. Wells, my name is Jake Kincannon, and I'm a close friend of your husband, Will. It is most important that I meet with you. Are you available for lunch?"

"Sir, I have never heard my husband speak of you."

"That may be. It was some time ago. But I assure you that it is most urgent. I'm happy to meet you in a public place so you can be assured that I'm not a crazy person. If what I have to say doesn't interest you, you are welcome to simply leave at anytime."

"Very well. I am working tomorrow, so I will have a visitor pass for you and meet you at the west entrance of the Pentagon. We can have coffee in the cafeteria. Can you be there at 1100 hours?"

"Absolutely. I will see you tomorrow, Saturday, at 1100, Pentagon west entrance. Good day."

"Good day, sir."

The next day, I arrived at the west entrance and looked for her. I had pictures of her with me from Doc. They were old pictures, and they looked it, but for her these were only weeks old. I spotted her immediately as she walked toward the entrance security desk where I was waiting.

"Hello, Mrs. Wells?"

She looked in my direction and walked smartly toward me. She was an extremely handsome woman, tall and shapely, but not like a model; she had some meat on her bones. Her blonde hair was shoulder length and styled for her time. It was real blonde too, not brash, bottle blonde. Her white blouse had a frilly collar and cuffs, her navy blue skirt hit her at midcalf, and her tan hose joined the skirt to her matching blue, high-heeled shoes.

"I'm glad you could meet with me." I held out my hand, and she shook it hesitantly.

"Mr. Kincannon, follow me please." Her voice was firm and cold.

I suspected she thought I was some kind of kook, but I was sure she felt safe with all the people moving about. Even for a Saturday, this place had many people walking to and fro. It was a fair distance to the cafeteria, where people in military uniforms and civilian clothes were beginning to gather for lunch. It looked like some of the cafeterias I had seen on military bases before. The chow line was manned with army personnel serving their selection of the day. The clanging of metal chairs added to the noise of a hundred different conversations going on between the patrons.

She pointed to a table, told me to sit there, and said she would get us coffee. I did as she suggested. I opened my briefcase and pulled out a thick manila folder and awaited her return. As she approached the table, carrying two mugs of coffee, I could see why Doc had sacrificed so much of his life to get her back. Yes, she was beautiful, but more than that, she was polished and poised. While she hadn't accepted me as a friend at this point, that wasn't important. My job was to save her life, not win a popularity contest.

"All right, Mr. Kincannon. Can you enlighten me as to what this visit is all about?" She still had enough of her German accent to give her a most distinctive and pleasant voice.

"I'd like to show you a few things that will make the fantastic story I'm about to tell you more believable. Frankly, ma'am, I'm now part of it, and I still find it hard to believe." I pulled out several photographs and handed them to her. "How old would you say these photos are?"

"Is this some kind of joke? I know these photos because Will took them only a couple of weeks ago. Yet if I didn't know them, I would say they are thirty or more years old."

"Forty-three years to be exact."

"Mr. Kincannon, this is ridiculous! What kind of game are you playing and for what purpose?"

I showed her a picture of Doc and myself taken for such purpose. "Do you recognize the people in this photo?"

She glared at me as she accepted the photo. "Yes, it's you and some older fellow. What is—"

"You don't know the older man? Look closely."

Once again, she glared hard into my eyes. She looked at the photo, studied it awhile, and then said, "Is that supposed to be Will?"

"Yes, in the year 1980."

She stood up quickly, knocking her chair over. A young marine sitting behind her picked it up. "Ma'am, are you okay?"

"Yes, Corporal, I'm fine. Thank you." She slowly sat back down. "Mr. Kincannon, why are you doing this?"

"Sheila, I don't know how to tell you this except to just say it. Your husband so loved you that he has spent the last forty-three years struggling to build a machine that could send someone, turns out to be me, back through time to save you from dying."

Her face became pale, and her shock at what I had just said was apparent on her face. "Mr. Kincannon, why would you perpetrate such a cruel hoax on me? What have I ever done to you? Hell, I don't even know you … do I?"

"No. I know of you only since meeting Doc, when he hired me to come back and save you so you and he would have a life together."

"Doc?"

"Oh, sorry. I mean Will. He goes by Doctor Wells, not Professor Wells, in my time, so that's how I've come to address him. He earned a PhD after you … well, later, but he did it for you. That's the important thing. You have a dedicated, loving, and loyal husband, Sheila."

She nodded as if she heard me loud and clear.

"He has sacrificed the last forty-three years building this machine to save you. Please let me do it for him … and you as well."

We continued to talk, and I showed her enough information that finally she seemed to believe me. At least enough that she agreed to stay home on May 10. I was very fortunate that she believed me before I had to use my trump card—the *Washington Post* front-page story about her death. I did inform her that I thought it best not to tell Doc anything about this, as he didn't need to know any details of the whole incident. I explained that when she didn't die, life would continue as usual. Doc would then never have to suffer the pain of knowing about how she died, and he would not have to carry the memories he had carried since that fateful day.

I told her she was kidnapped, mugged, and killed, but I left out the morbid details of her death, and she didn't ask. While I found that a little strange, I was thankful for it. I would later come to regret my strategy. She asked me many questions about Doc, and I answered all I could.

Finally she asked me a question that was very perceptive: "If Doc doesn't know about the time machine business, how will you get back after history changes?"

I answered her query with another: "How do you know so much about this subject?"

She laughed for the first time. "The same reason you do … Will."

"Doc," I said at the same time as if to answer my own query. I remembered that Doc had said he had been fascinated with that subject since he was a kid. In fact, it was part of the reason he had pursued the educational path that he did.

Her laugh matched the rest of her, and I knew Doc was a very lucky man to have found her. She told me she also knew of his childhood dreams on the subject and that in his classroom he had a sign above the chalkboard behind his desk that read, *Space travel and time travel will happen through science and wonder.* Then she said she had to return to work, and she actually gave me a hug, so she must have believed me.

"Sheila, now you promise me you will not report to the Pentagon next Monday the tenth?"

She laughed again. "I promise. In fact, you can come by the house Monday around one o'clock for tea and crumpets if you like."

"I would like that very much, but I don't want Doc to meet me."

"Oh, don't worry. He has class on Monday. That's his long day, and he won't be home until around six."

"Oh, well then, that would be quite nice." After all, what else did I have to do?

"Great. Here's my address. See you then. Good day."

"Good day, Sheila." I watched her walk away, and it was at that moment that I was glad I had accepted Doc's assignment. I wasn't looking at her in any romantic or sexual way, just in wonder and joy for Doc, as he would soon recoup the lost forty-three years with her instead of being locked up in that basement, inventing that machine. I was sure glad that he had left himself the exact details, plans, and schematics on how to quickly build the machine to bring me home. I also told her about the footlockers and their location and why it was critical she tell Doc and make him look at their contents. My safe return back to the present was relying on that.

As I took my cab ride back to the city, I had nothing but time until dark, and I had brought along my 35mm camera, so I decided to play your average American tourist. I had the cabby drop me at Fourteenth Street, opposite the Washington Monument, and started my photo taking. I walked some and took short cab rides to other landmarks before heading back toward my hotel, enjoying the warm summer day and the sights of this most famous city.

Since I was in no hurry, I zigged and zagged through the streets to capture for forever as many notable sights as possible to take back to my time. Eventually shooting up my two rolls of film, I began navigating my way back to my hotel with the help of a few strangers to guide my way. It seemed I had gotten myself lost following the landmarks.

As I meandered back toward my home away from home, I thought of how DC was so different from my hometown of Chicago, prettier in some ways with grand, important buildings and monuments like the Capitol Building, the Washington and Lincoln Monuments, and the White House, not to mention the large areas of well-manicured lawns. But I already missed my Chi-town with its skyscrapers and miles of waterfront, and yes, I had to admit, it was Julie that I was really missing.

I didn't need to be daydreaming at a time like this, so I ducked into a restaurant and had a really late lunch. I took my time and ate a leisurely meal. It was a nice change from the usual gobble-down-type lunches I usually had. Afterward, I went back to my room. It had begun to sprinkle rain, and I didn't have enough clothes to get these soaked.

After reaching the hotel lobby, just as it started to pour cats and dogs, I stopped at the front desk and asked for them to give me a wake-up call at 1730 hours. I had to be at the beam point at 1800 on the dot. I had decided to take a nap, a luxury I usually didn't afford myself before dinner. I slept soundly, and after what seemed like just minutes, the phone rang. Still a little groggy from my nap, I hit the shower and then headed out for dinner. But first I walked back to the parking lot.

Doc, in his note, had changed the beam point because the street would have been far too crowded at 1800 to have something materialize out of thin air. I couldn't draw suspicion to myself, so I was to go to the parking lot at the rear of the building, at an exact spot where a white box would appear. I had to set the tube there and remember exactly where the spot was, as that would be my beam-out point. I arrived two minutes before, and at precisely 1800, the expected white box from Doc arrived. I placed the tube on the exact spot, and poof, it was gone, and poof, it was back. I saw that Doc had put in five hundred dollars' worth of bills that were properly dated, and I sent back all the money I had on me that was not of this time. I waited for the empty tube to return. Now I could rest easy that I wouldn't spend the next twenty years in prison for counterfeiting.

I decided to eat at the restaurant in the hotel that night because it was still raining off and on. I had been seated next to the window for only moments when it really began to pour. I sat in comfort sipping a martini, my usual before-dinner drink, and watched people running for cover. I was relaxed, my martini was good, and my meal was okay but not spectacular, so after dinner I walked outside. The rain had now tapered off to a mere mist, and I wanted to go a couple rounds with my favorite bourbon to aid my sleep. I rationalized that I had earned it. So I crossed the street to the bar for a nightcap before going back to my room.

When I walked into the bar, it looked much like most bars of my day—dimly lit and smoky. The bartender was tending to his customers seated along the bar. Waitresses were waiting on the tables. Everyone was talking and laughing, and they generally seemed to be having a good time. I settled onto the barstool at the end of the bar. I noticed a big clock above the bar; it had an hour, minute, and second hand, but no numbers. How strange I thought that was. I studied the positions of the hands of the clock, and it seemed to indicate the time was about 1935. I checked my wrist watch … close enough.

The bar's décor was slightly different and, I guessed, typical of its time, but what stood out more than anything else was the music coming from the jukebox. It was atypical compared to what I was used to and had caught my ear the moment I opened the door. It was mostly big band and crooners. It was the music of the day, but not my day, which was mostly disco. As the bartender poured my second Jack Daniels, a rather tall brunette slid onto the vacant stool beside me.

"Got a light, stranger?"

I retrieved my Zippo from my pocket and torched her smoke. She caressed my lighter-holding hand and stared into my eyes as she sucked in the flame to her cigarette. I knew what she wanted, and I wondered what a little trip like that would cost.

"Thank you, kind sir. My name is Crystal Malone."

"I'm Jake Kincannon. Pleased to meet you, and you are quite welcome," I said, admiring her as I spoke.

She wore a skirt that was slit up to her garter and a blouse that revealed that she was braless. I didn't know women went out like that in that era, but on the other hand, it was the oldest profession. But don't get me wrong; this was no off-the-street, uneducated, pimp-owned, average-looking hooker. This was the grand-a-night class in my day. Fortunately for me, if I was interested, this was the thirties.

She bought me a drink and then another. I should have refused and left when I wasn't interested. However, I didn't, and we drank and talked about many things, but I had to be careful what I said. This was the longest conversation I'd had with anyone save Sheila on this side of time, and it was very difficult. I always had to be on guard so something unheard of in her time wouldn't slip from my slightly buzzed brain and roll off the end of my tongue.

"So where are you from, Jake?"

"Chicago."

"Here on business?"

"Yes."

I had to think quickly of the answer to the next query, but she didn't ask it. Instead she asked where I was staying, and when she found out it was next door, she kept hinting that I should invite her up for a nightcap. I thought of Julie and then rationalized that she wasn't even born yet. This woman was very seductive in her look, her speech, and her touchy manner. Her fingers with red polished nails found my leg many noticeable times.

I remembered a saying I once heard when I was visiting Las Vegas: *what happens in Vegas stays in Vegas.* And I thought that must go double in 1937. I mean, come on. I wasn't just out of town. I was out of time!

So I stood up and threw a ten on the bar. "Shall we?"

A big smile crossed her face. She nodded and winked at the bartender, and out we went. Now that was what's known as either an unintended consequence or benefit. Only the dawn would tell me which. It would be almost dawn before the evening's activities were over. The night was most enjoyable, and when the dawn came, we were both asleep and would be for several more hours.

When we woke Sunday, we showered together and had each other one last time. Room service brought us a late breakfast, and when it came time for her to leave ... well, let me just say it was a good thing Doc sent me as much as he did. As I took a long look at her walking away, and as she moved farther and farther away, the guilt of my deeds slowly slipped into my brain, and I had to tolerate the torture of it all.

Boredom and guilt filled the rest of the day. After all, how much radio can one listen to? I went for a long walk under threat of rain, but fortunately it didn't. Finally, as I returned toward my hotel, I stopped for dinner and had a martini before and a brandy after and nothing to look forward to for the rest of the evening. I suffered through Monday morning until finally it was time to go for tea with Sheila. I hoped our visit would give me some relief from my guilty feelings about giving in to Crystal.

Once I was properly dressed, it was time for a cab ride to the Wells' residence in Alexandria. They lived in an area known as Fort Hunt, very near George Washington's home at Mount Vernon. It was a nice ride along the Potomac River. Staring out the cab window at the river's gently rolling current and the monuments on the other side, one could conjure up images of George Washington crossing the Potomac. Presidents like Washington, Monroe, Madison, and Franklin came to mind, along with the proud heritage of a band of countrymen who had a dream to be free and independent and to create a country based on those principles.

As I daydreamed about those early days of our country, I knew many Americans in this time were worried about the war Germany had started in Europe and how long the United States could stay out. Some probably wondered what would happen if we were to lose. I knew the outcome but had no way to tell them or allay their fears. The braking of the cab as it came to a stop shook me back to the present. As I stood at the door of Doc's house, I knew I was once again about to see the woman whose life was so important to a man that he would give up his future for her rescue. He had but one simple belief and goal, which was that he could conquer time, the fourth dimension. And by golly, he did it.

The door opened, and there she was. She was as lovely and proper as she could be. As the afternoon progressed, I came to know that Sheila was as fine and beautiful on the inside as she was on the outside. In the quiet of the house, I picked up the slight traces of her German accent again, which I had noticed in the noisy cafeteria but could more clearly enjoy now. I liked the sound of her voice; it was very distinctive. In a way, she sort of reminded me of Julie. They didn't look alike or sound alike, but inside they seemed very similar. Damn, when I thought of Julie, I thought of what I had done the night before. Sometimes I can be so stupid.

She served the tea in fine china that, from its markings, looked like it must be old and from the Rhine country. I also noticed other things that must have come from her native Germany as I looked around her finely decorated home. I was now even more determined to see her safely into the future—a future that had been denied to her for these many years.

I chuckled a bit. "Sheila, when I see you next, you will be quite different."

"How so … other than age?"

"That's just it. It will be as if this was an old movie I was watching, and then it will be like seeing the actress in a later time."

"But I will now have years with Will that I didn't have, and all thanks to him and to you."

We talked about things of my time, which she was curious about, and of her years as a youngster in Germany.

"Now, Jake, tell me this: Will we actually go to war with Germany?"

"Now, if you remember anything Doc told you, then you know I can't answer that. It could cause you to do something different and change history."

She seemed disturbed and pleased at the same time, so I quickly changed the subject.

We had a great afternoon together, one I would never forget.

When the time came for me to leave, I knew several things I hadn't known before. Sheila was an excellent homemaker and a gracious hostess. She was a caring person and made excellent crumpets. Well, actually they weren't crumpets but something she called cherry *kuchen*. They were delicious. She and Doc had a beautiful home in a private and secluded part of the suburbs. Most importantly, she didn't go to work that day, and now history was changed. The cab arrived to take me back to the hotel at 1600. I thanked my hostess and told her not to forget how she made that cherry stuff, as I wanted more when I saw her in 1980.

She laughed. "I'll make a tray of it special for you when I see you then."

I knew that would be a real experience. She would tell Doc the whole story upon her return home the night she didn't die. Sheila would know me, but Doc would not, at least until he opened the trunk and read its contents. I hoped she would make the whys and wherefores clear. In 1937, Sheila is twenty-six years of age, and I've transported back in time at my present age of thirty-two. If somehow Doc got it into his head that there was any funny business between us, I would likely live out my life in this era.

We hugged and said our good-byes, and I hopped into the cab. As the cab headed back up along the Potomac, I was absolutely elated, almost giddy with the prospect of having saved a life that meant so much to my friend Doc. I discovered that a euphoric high was better than any alcoholic buzz you could get. How cool it was that by midnight I would step onto the beam point and within seconds would be back in my time, and there would be Doc as I had left him and a much older Sheila than I had come to know and appreciate. I wondered if she would still be as nice of a person as I had come to know.

The part that was going to be strange was that within a few hours of my return, everything would change. I mean everything. I wondered how she would age. Gracefully and painlessly, I hoped. Would she have a tray of cherry kuchen waiting for me, or would that memory have faded over forty-three years? My mind filled with all the possibilities as I rode along and again watched the Potomac River slowly flow by. I wondered about how all this time travel and changing history stuff really worked. It made sense to me that history was actually changing from the moment I called

Sheila's and got her to agree to see me. Very subtly at first and perhaps without noticeable consequences.

By 1625, I was back in my room, and I was exhausted but excited. I turned on the radio and lay across the bed. My only remaining job was to be at the beam point by midnight, and the rest, as they say, would be history. Or should I say a new history for a small group of people? And what a new significance that had for me now. I called the front desk for a wake-up call at 2345. I couldn't miss my flight. *Flight?* That struck me as funny, as I would never see an airport. I began to laugh aloud. I must have still been a bit euphoric. That feeling would abruptly end seconds after midnight when I stepped on the beam point.

Chapter 11

WRONG PLACE, WRONG TIME

The best way to kill time was to sleep, so I got up, kicked off my shoes, unbuttoned my shirt, and loosened my belt. Peeling back the covers and fluffing the pillow was essential to a nice nap. However, sleep didn't come.

What I had thought would be a nice nap to kill the time between now and my midnight rendezvous didn't happen. I couldn't sleep because my brain wouldn't shut down—an extremely rare occasion for me. I couldn't get three women out of my mind. The first was Julie, and what I had done with the second woman I couldn't get clear of my brain, and the third was Sheila and what the new reality would bring for her.

Finally, sleep must have come, as I was awakened by the wake-up call. It was 2345 and time for me to go. The hotel bill was paid, so I left the key on the dresser, and within minutes I was at the beam point, ready to step on in two minutes. I watched the second hand of my watch move toward the bewitching hour, and I stepped onto the spot. I was trying to prepare myself for the loss of memory and the stomach lift when suddenly I felt the lift and then heard the sound of the machine's noise winding down. I was back in the machine in Doc's laboratory. My memory was intact, thank goodness! A few seconds later, I saw Doc looking through the porthole as he spun the hatch handle.

The second I stepped out of the machine, before I could say a word, he was pressing me for information.

"Well ... what happened? Come on, man. Give!"

"Whoa, Doc. Slow down. Let me catch my breath. I was with her at your home until 1600. She had promised not to go to work and proved it to me by having me for tea."

Doc looked at me funny. "Where was I?"

"It was your long day in class, remember?"

"Hell no, I don't remember. That was a lifetime ago. Tell me, man, how was she? How'd she look? What did you do? What did she say?"

I began to laugh at Doc, and through the laughter, I said, "Doc, one question at a time."

Doc must have realized how silly he sounded, so he cleared his throat. "Quite right, quite right."

I told him everything, including my plan to leave him out of my plan. I answered all his questions as we waited for things to change. Neither of us knew where we would end up. He would have built the new Teleporter somewhere else, and the ripple of history could instantly have us wherever that somewhere else was. This had never been done before. We reasoned that Julie's life and mine would be unchanged as I was transporting for only a brief time out of that life and back into it. Then I would return to a world unchanged but enhanced by the existence of Sheila and however that changed their lifestyle. But the only change for Julie and I would be enjoying the one hundred grand in our account.

We talked and laughed in anticipation of what would happen at approximately 0200 on May 11, 1937. We were like two guys counting the minutes and seconds until the start of the New Year. We actually did, but when we got to the part where people would be screaming "Happy New Year," we just stared at each other.

"What! Doc, you're still here … I'm still here! What happened?"

"Well, remember the coroner's time of death was an estimate. It could have been up to two hours later that she actually died."

"Oh, I see."

We went back to talking, certain that at any moment we would be whisked away to a different place with all new memories. Perhaps only I would have any memory of this, and maybe Sheila also. At 0300, still no Sheila. We noticed when the cuckoo clock recorded the time and then went on talking, waiting anxiously for something to happen. It didn't. Finally, Doc said something must have gone wrong. I tried to rationalize that we just needed to wait a little longer. I was pacing now.

"Sit down, Jake. Let's try to figure this out."

I rejoined him at the table. "Doc, I don't understand. Could this mean that I saved her and she subsequently died before 1980?"

"No, Jake, because I have no memory of that, and I would if she had lived longer than 1937. Plus, that would have changed many things too. No, something else went wrong. Tell me everything that happened. Don't leave out anything."

"Okay. Well, I landed in 1937, just as you said I would, even the exact date and time."

I continued with all the exact details as accurately as possible. We went back and forth for hours until neither of us could keep our eyes open. We literally fell asleep at the table. The elevator operator ringing the line awakened us. When Doc answered it, it was Julie, worried about why I hadn't come home last night as planned.

Doc let her come down, and she jumped into my arms when she saw me. At that moment, I really wished I could have undone what I did with Crystal. I felt like a real heel. Hell, I *was* a real heel! Julie and I hugged and kissed until Doc, growing impatient, cleared his throat like one does when he or she wants your attention. We got the point.

"Sorry Doc. Doc, this is Julie Carson, and Julie, meet Doctor Wilson Wells." After the usual pleasantries, Julie looked at Doc. "Where's the kitchen? You boys need some coffee."

Doc just pointed, and off she went.

"Jake, I figured it out. Sheila either went to work after you left her—"

"Impossible, Doc. Why would she go there? Even if she left shortly after I did, it would have been almost 1700 by the time she got there. Who goes to work to arrive at quitting time?"

"Maybe she forgot something, and she went to get it, or perhaps she didn't die as the papers recorded, or they got the date wrong. Maybe she was killed in an auto accident, a burglary. Anything could be the real history."

"Stop, Doc. I know where this is going. You want me to go back and find out what went wrong and fix it, right?"

"There is no other way. We've come too close to stop now. After all, you are the detective. You will have to track down why the history didn't change."

Then a voice from across the room said, "Yes, you have to go back."

Doc and I turned to see Julie standing there with a pot of coffee and two mugs in her hands. She had a solemn look on her beautiful face.

"That a girl. See, Jake. She is smarter than you!"

"Honey, are you sure?"

"Yes. I know how I would feel if you were killed and someone had a chance to save you. Plus, now you have gone and come back, so I'm not afraid anymore. Doc knows what he's doing."

"Okay, I'll go back. Besides, Doc, I know why you have labored so hard to bring her back."

Doc threw his fists on his hips and wrinkled up his face. "You damn well better not know *all* the reasons!"

Julie got it first and began to laugh, and that got me laughing, which in turn got Doc laughing. It was a moment of humor we all needed. Julie poured us some coffee, and we toasted my return to the past. Then Julie went back to the kitchen and whipped up some eggs and toast for the three of us. As we ate, I thought about how determined I was to solve this new wrinkle, change history, and save Sheila. Also, I still wanted Doc to have no memory of her death. When I figured it out—and I would figure it out—he would think she came home from work that fateful night, just like every night before that. I told him I would call him in the morning and let him know what time I would be ready to return but that now Julie and I had some catching up to do.

"Oh, honey, let me clean up the dishes from breakfast first."

"No, no. You kids run along. I'll take care of all that. Go on, get out of here," Doc said, using a shooing motion to let us know he was serious and that he understood.

We took our leave of him and strolled back to the office arm in arm, and man did she feel good to me. She got her things, and we headed for home, and you can probably imagine where we spent the rest of the day. That evening, we went out to dinner at our favorite restaurant and had some nice wine and a fine dinner of steak and lobster. We had a little brandy after dinner, and then we returned home for some more togetherness.

As we drove home, I thought about what Doc had explained before. He said *when* I was successful. Interestingly, he never said *if* I was successful. It was always *when* I was successful. The last recovery beam on my next mission would be at 0145, and it would beam me back into my office, as his laboratory wouldn't exist. This was the part I had some trouble with initially, because if I couldn't get back on the last flight, he wouldn't have built the Teleporter, and I'd be stranded in history.

However, he reassured me that he would be motivated to build it because of all the detailed information he left for himself that Sheila would be sure he'd find. My life would change, as I would not receive the phone call that started all this, because of all that would be different when I returned. But it could be like two different memories for the same time period for Julie and me only. When I was successful, I would most likely see Doc *and* Sheila upon my return. But what would that reunion be like? Who would remember what? Would Sheila tell him where to find the plans and that he needed to build it if I missed the last flight? My mind was whirling with all that might come to pass or not, and it would all be based on whether I saved Sheila's life or not. This time travel stuff was way too confusing for me.

CHAPTER 12

MORE TRAVELING THROUGH TIME

The next morning, it was back to Doc's and a return to the past in search of what had gone wrong on the first mission. This would be a really quick trip. Doc was right; there were only a couple possible explanations. I favored the idea that she didn't die as the papers had reported, and that was where I would start. If the first assumption was true, then there would most likely be something Sheila had left out, either because she thought it was insignificant or because she was deliberately withholding something. Based on what I knew of her, I favored the former. After all, why would she need to conceal anything?

After I reached Doc's and took the mysterious elevator ride to his lair, I found him all shook up from what he said was fear we would not find her. I reassured him that I would go back as many times as it took to figure it out … as long as his money held out, of course. He got a slight chuckle out of that.

"Say, Doc. I need a small favor. Can you send me back for an hour? I need to correct something personal, and I don't want you to inquire about it. Can you do that?"

"No, I'm afraid not. You see, my power source is not infinite, and I have only a small amount, enough for only a few more trips, and I don't know how long it will take to acquire more. Maybe if I can procure more, we can do it then. Okay?"

"Sure, Doc. I understand," I said. "Well, let's get the show on the road. I have a lot of investigating to do."

"Quite right, Jake, quite right." He freshened up my stash of period-correct bread and clothes, and I was ready to go.

It was 1030 hours in Chicago, and the time was set for me to arrive back in DC on Monday, May 10, 1937, at 1200, high noon. This time, I again felt the stomach lift but suffered no memory loss when I landed. When I materialized back in time, I saw the maintenance man washing his truck. Fortunately, he had his back to me and was unaware of my materializing and my presence.

I walked over to him. "Hello."

He turned sharply. "Oh, Mr. Kincannon. You startled me. Thought you had left us?"

"Yes, but my plans were suddenly changed, and I need to stay longer. Say, how do you know me?"

"Oh, when you were here before, you had asked the lady at the front desk about Pearl Harbor, and she asked me, and I didn't know either, so we looked it up in the encyclopedia, and she pointed you out to me when you came back, and she told you where it was."

"Oh, I see, and what is your name?" as I extended my hand.

"Henry, sir, Henry Miller."

"Nice to know you Henry. Listen, Henry. I need a big favor. Would you loan me your truck this evening?"

"Oh no, sir. I couldn't risk that. I need it for my job."

Of course he wouldn't, so I asked him if he would rent it to me, and I showed him a one-hundred-dollar bill.

He grabbed the bill and said, "Sure thing, mister. Just don't use it to kill anyone." Then he laughed.

I joined in the laughter and slapped him on the back. We worked out the details and exchanged the keys for the money. Then I went to the lobby to check in again.

"Gee, mister, plans changed, huh?"

I thought everyone was sure curious about my comings and goings, so I figured I'd give her a good story. "Well, there's this girl, see. And she lives about fifty miles from here, and well, she wanted me to spend some time with her, but it seems our visit got cut short, if you follow me."

She winked and smiled. "Indeed I do, sir. Indeed I do."

She took my money and handed me my key. "Now, you just let me know if you need anything, anything at all." She winked again.

I thanked her and quickly went to my room to drop my bag off. Then I took the truck and drove to Sheila's house. I had planned to get a taxi to take me there, but Henry's truck made things easier. It was quite a simple plan, really. Everything I had done on my first trip remained unchanged. I would take Henry's truck and be waiting across the street at the same time I left the house on the last trip. Then I could observe her and find out what happened after I left her and why history was not as it was reported to be. The time was now 1630.

I had barely cut the engine when her car pulled out of the garage. She was driving, apparently alone. I slipped down in the seat to remain unseen and then followed her at a safe distance.

The newspaper's account of what had happened was obviously wrong and appeared very fishy, and I was going to learn the truth about all of it. When I was successful, history would not be repeated because I would change it forever. Doc and Sheila would have their life together. I could only speculate as to where she was about to lead me and to what outcome, but it wasn't long before I knew where she was headed—the Pentagon. She parked her car and just sat in it. I parked two rows back and observed. The time of her reported abduction had now passed by forty-five minutes. Actually, we didn't even arrive until shortly after her reported abduction. Something was clearly amiss.

Surely she knew she was going to die, but I, having been misled, also misled her. She thought she was going to be kidnapped and murdered. My account of her death had led her to an erroneous conclusion that it was now safe to do whatever she had planned. Clearly the killer was not some random opportunist but someone else. Someone the military or that particular soldier wanted covered up … but why?

Another twenty minutes went by. Suddenly, she opened her car door as a black limo approached and then stopped. She got into the back of it, and it began to pull away. I followed. I couldn't help but notice that she was dressed in evening wear. Interesting. I wrote down the tag number at the first stoplight. The limo headed into DC and pulled up in front of the Mayflower Hotel, where she got out and entered. It took me several minutes to find a parking place, and by the time I reached the lobby, she was gone. I searched the bar and restaurant but had no luck. I asked the front desk, but they did not recall a woman of my description checking in.

I waited in the lobby for five hours until a hotel detective started toward me with that look of suspicion, or at least that was how I interpreted it. I couldn't take the chance, so I looked at my watch, for his benefit, acted as though I had been stood up, and casually walked out the side entrance. I returned to my hotel, grabbed a quick bite, and returned Henry's truck.

"Here she is, Henry. Not a scratch on her."

"Thank you, Mr. Kincannon. I appreciate that."

"Henry, you wouldn't by chance know anyone in law enforcement, would you?"

A big smile came over his face, and he said proudly, "Yes, sir. My brother."

"Henry, you're full of surprises! Do you think you could get him to tell me to whom this license plate is registered?" I handed him the paper with the number, and he went to the phone. He returned ten minutes later and said the limo belonged to the Ackerson Limo Service, and he had taken the liberty of calling and had gotten them to tell him it was currently rented to the German embassy.

"Henry, you're worth your weight in gold!"

There was little I could do, and my time was running short. I went to my room, waited until 2345, and then headed for the beam point. Sheila would still be dead by morning, with the only difference being she died knowing a strange visitor from another time. However, this time I had a really good clue to work with, and yes, I would have to return again, hopefully for the final time, to save her. I was kind of getting used to the time travel stuff. After all, no one in the whole wide world has logged more time travel than yours truly.

I returned to the beam point for my red-eye flight back to Doc's laboratory and, unfortunately, another unsuccessful trip to the other side of time. Once again, when I felt that stomach lifting sensation, I knew I was on my way through time, though the trip was almost instantaneous. I opened my eyes, and there I was looking out the porthole of the pod at a very inquisitive-looking Doc. I saw his shoulders lean from left to right as he turned the wheel that sealed the pod door. It opened, and I was back in my time in one piece.

His eyes seemed like giant question marks, so I jumped right in. "Doc, she won't be coming through, but I have some great clues I must track down in this time period."

I told him all the details of this trip, answered every query, and made sure he was satisfied. "Doc, I have to get home and start working on this first thing in the morning."

"Quite right, Jake. Do it, and let's get her back. Thanks. You're doing great!"

I changed back into the clothes I'd worn to Doc's lab and ran to my office, where I hoped I would find Julie. As the elevator stopped and opened, I took a deep breath, straightened my tie, and walked to my office door. As I looked through the glass, I could see her sitting at her desk, typing something. I felt a smile creep over my face. One of the fringe benefits of this crazy time travel was that I could compress time. So even though I left 1937 at midnight, I arrived back home at 1300. She stopped to take a sip of coffee, and our eyes caught. I pushed through the door as she ran to me.

She hugged me and whispered, "Oh, Jake, I missed you so much!"

I told her I had thought of her every minute I was away. Now that's an interesting point about time travel. I was there, 1937, in real time; in other words, for each hour I spent in 1937, sixty real minutes of time elapsed. Yet I returned in three hours of 1980 time. It had something to do with the warping of time. I didn't really understand it, but that was how it worked. We kissed and pulled back just enough to look into each other's eyes. Then we kissed again and again. I think I could have just kept kissing her all day, but there was serious work to get done.

Finally, she broke away and said, "Well, tell me all about this trip. Successful?"

"No, baby, but I think I have the clues to solve it, and I'll need your help."

"No problem. Girl Friday is always ready." She gave me a wink and a salute.

She listened as she poured me a cup of coffee and handed it gently to me. I told her everything, including my second failure to save Doc's wife. Then I told her I had to go back and try again. But she was used to it by now; this would be trip number three and hopefully the last. They say the third time's a charm. I hoped they were right. I told her of my suspicions, but the real detective work now had to be done. I guessed Doc was pretty smart after all, choosing a PI for his go-between. However, before I could travel through time again, I had to first travel by air. A flight to the nation's capital, and man if you thought Chicago politicians are crooked, wait until we get a load of DC!

I gave her the phone number for an old friend. I thought he could help us out. I asked her to track him down. I had a plan, but it would require help from afar. Good to her job, she quickly ran down Bob Dawson, a former Chicago detective I had partnered with just before I left the force. He had left Chicago to be with his family back in Arlington and had joined the Arlington County PD as a homicide detective. Then he was promoted to lieutenant in charge of the cold case division. Who would have ever guessed that one day in the future, he would help me try to solve a case that was really cold? We had a nice long chat, and he agreed to help me in any way he could. That was music to my ears, so I thanked him and told him I'd see him as fast as I could get there.

I asked Julie to call the airline and book two round-trip tickets to Washington, DC, on the first flight out in the morning, if not sooner. I also told her to get us a room at a motel near Washington National Airport.

"Who's the second ticket for?"

"It's for you, silly. Who did you think?"

"What! We're going to the nation's capital?"

"We sure are, babe. Just as fast as we can book a flight, pack a bag, and get to O'Hare."

She was so excited, but I cautioned her that this was work, not some sightseeing adventure. I would be working hard on this case until we found out why the newspaper reports didn't match reality.

"Julie, tell the answering service the office will be closed for a few days and we'll call in for messages."

I then called Doc and asked him to try to think of anything, anything that might give some additional insight to the case—no matter how insignificant he might think it was—and let me know ASAP. I told him we were going to DC to find out the truth about Sheila. Then we could change history and save her from her fate. I told him I would also let him know where we were staying after I arrived in Washington.

After Doc and I spoke, Julie informed me, "We've got two tickets on the red-eye for tonight."

"That's great, babe. Let's finish up here, get a bite on the way to the house, and go pack. Perhaps we can get a little shut-eye before we leave for the airport."

Everything went as planned, and shortly after midnight we were boarding our flight. This was my first visit to Washington—in the modern era, that is. It was also Julie's first time. I wondered how different it would look after forty-three years. Time would tell. I also hoped we would be able to find out who Sheila had gone to visit that day. I had to come back to the reality of my time that traveling across country was much slower than traveling back through time. I guess when the reality of *Star Trek* comes, we can just beam ourselves from place to place.

I hoped my friend there would be the ace up my sleeve. The Pentagon sat within the border of his county. Although his department didn't have jurisdiction over the Pentagon, I believed Bob could give us the help we needed.

Bob would now get his chance to help. Shortly after he joined the force, some Arlington County homicide detectives had been fired for being caught up in some nefarious doings. They had wanted to bring in fresh blood, so to speak, to clean things up. Bob had only been there a month, and that's how he got snagged. Now a lieutenant, he had been made head of that division. They handled cold cases. I was deep in thought, and when I looked over at Julie, I saw she was already asleep. I dozed in and out through the duration of the flight, and once we were on the ground, a cab took us to a nice motel on Jefferson Davis Highway. This would be our home base until we discovered the truth about that night when Sheila wasn't where she was supposed to be and ended up taking an early morning plunge into the Potomac River.

CHAPTER 13

A VISIT WITH AN OLD FRIEND

We slept in until about 1100, and we had barely finished dressing when there was a loud knock at the door. I knew that knock. That was the knock of a cop, so it had to be Bob. I told Julie it would be easier if we just told him we were married. She nodded and, being one sharp gal, took her grandmother's wedding ring off her right ring finger and quickly moved it to her left ring finger.

I opened the door, and there he was, all six foot seven of him, still sporting the white sidewalls from his days in the marine corps. Bob looked like he could be a professional football player. He was tall and built like a tank. He came in, and we shook hands and then hugged. I introduced him to my wife, and we exchanged the usual small talk and did a little catching up. Then we got to it.

"Jake, let's get down to brass tacks. What did you need my help with?"

"Bob, a good friend of mine lost his wife forty-three years ago in a brutal rape that ended in her death. The official report was that a person or persons unknown had kidnapped her as she was walking through the parking lot at the Pentagon to her car early one evening. The kidnapper was driving a black panel truck. It seems an army sergeant was the lone witness who saw her being pulled into the truck, but it sped away before he could get close enough to get a license plate number. She worked as a civilian employee at the Pentagon, and that was where she was abducted."

"So how can I help you with that?"

"Her body washed up on and was discovered on your side of the river, in Arlington County. So you would have had jurisdiction in that case.

Now, here's where it gets interesting. New information reveals that she was not abducted as it was reported, but she actually knew her assailant and got willingly into a limo that was leased by the German embassy in the Pentagon visitors' parking lot when she was abducted. I am asking you, with my help, of course, to reopen the case and help me find out what really happened."

"I don't know about this, man. Power is always an issue, and it seems this could take many, many man-hours with the case as old as it is."

"I thought you might say that, but again, you'll have Julie's help and mine. We'll carry as much of the load as possible. I just need you to open doors for me and get me whatever exists in that case file. Julie and I are going to the morgues of the local papers, the *Post* and the *Star*, to gather whatever they have. I need you to get me the name and whereabouts of the lone witness. Also, if we need any info from the Pentagon, this case will need to be officially opened to garner their cooperation."

"Well, I see you haven't forgotten your police work. All right, I'll do it. But I can't spend any man-hours but my own, and that may have to be on my own time. At least until we get something solid to go on. Good thing there's no statute of limitations on murder."

"That's for sure. Thanks, Bob. You don't know what this means to me."

"By the way, Jake, why are you so interested in this case? Was she a relative?"

"No. She is, or should I say was, the wife of a very dear friend of mine, and when he discovered this new information, he hired me to find out the truth. He needs to be at peace with this again, as he was before he learned this new truth."

"Okay. Let me get back to the office and get this case officially reopened, and I'll drop off a copy of the file on my way home tonight."

"Thanks again, Bob. I really appreciate it."

"It's okay. What are pals for? But it will cost you dinner before you go home."

"You got it. I'd love to see your lovely wife again anyway. So long. See you later."

After Bob left, Julie and I went for lunch. She insisted. She knew that if I got hungry, I got very grouchy. While at lunch, we discussed our itinerary for the afternoon. From there, she went to the *Evening Star*, and I headed for the *Washington Post* to search their morgue sections for all we could find on the murder and any social info on either Doc or Sheila.

"Julie, you'll be looking for Professor Wells."

"I thought you said he was Dr. Wells."

"Not in 1937 he wasn't."

"Oh, I see."

We then met back at the motel. Julie arrived first, and when I got there, she told me there had been a message for me at the front desk. She handed it to me. It read:

> *A Bob Dawson called and said the man you wanted to*
> *meet was John Campbell. His last known address was*
> *1404 N. 15th Street, Arlington, Virginia.*

"Interesting. Let's take a run over there." Before the words were completely out of my mouth, Julie was dialing the phone for a cab.

We soon arrived at the doorstep of the address Bob had given us. I knocked, and an older gentleman answered the door.

"Yes, may I help you?"

"Yes, sir. Are you John Campbell?"

He looked at me strangely and paused, "May I ask what you want with John Campbell?"

I pulled my PI badge and showed it to him, "Sir my name is Jake Kincannon, and this is my assistant Julie Carson. We have been hired to find information about a kidnapping that John Campbell witnessed."

He looked at me and then at Julie and back at me again, "Come in, please."

He led us to the living room of his old frame, Victorian-style home and offered us a seat.

"Would you like something to drink?"

We declined.

"My name is Harold Campbell. May I ask why you wish to see my brother and how you know him?"

"Well, it seems that forty-three years ago he was a witness to a kidnapping while he was stationed at the Pentagon. The case of the murder victim has been reopened by the Arlington County Police."

"Are you police officers?"

"No, sir. I'm a private investigator from Chicago, and this is Julie, my assistant. We're here on behalf of a client. Is your brother at home?"

His face, which had been rather cautious but pleasant up to that point, became red, and he seemed highly agitated.

"My brother is in an army hospital in Baltimore, where he has been since one month after the incident you spoke of. It seems, according to the military, that he had a nervous breakdown after witnessing the event and then finding out that she was killed in a most foul way. He's no more mentally ill than I am, but I can't fight the military."

"Sir, is there any way I could talk with him?"

"He isn't allowed any visitors except family, and I'm the only family he has left. His wife divorced him after he was sent to that institution."

"Can you get me into speak to him? I could be a nephew—no, that wouldn't work. I was born after John was stuck in that place. Who could I be, Mr. Campbell?"

"Now hold on, Mr. Kincannon. Is there any way that you going to see him might help get him released?"

"I can't say for certain, but I'll use all my skill and contacts to help him. I'm responsible for reopening the case."

"Well … I have a son, Corey, who lives overseas now and has never seen Johnny. You could be him, and since you're offering to do more than anyone else has offered to do, I'm willing to give it a try. Yes, by golly, it might work. I was planning a visit next week, but perhaps I can move it up some." He reached for a pad and pencil. "Here's my phone number. Call me tomorrow after noontime, and I'll let you know what I have arranged."

I gave him our hotel number as well, and we thanked him and returned to the hotel in the waiting cab.

"Well, it's a lead, which is more than we had before."

Julie took my hand in hers and rested her head on my shoulder. Her mouth was close to my ear. Her breath tickled my ear as she spoke softly so as to not engage the cab driver in our conversation.

"I know you'll find out what happened to Sheila, and Doc will be grateful, and he'll also expect you to return for a third time to save her. I want her to live, but I wish it wasn't you taking all the risk. I must tell you that I've been unable to shake the feeling that if you return to the past and save her, I'll never see you again. Never! I know Doc has assured you that won't happen, and you've explained the safeguards to me. I felt a little better about these trips after you returned safely from the first trip. Still, I fear the unknown of the change of history.

"I feel ashamed for being so selfish, but I love you, and I can't help it. If Sheila doesn't die, we have no idea how the future will turn on that one slight change. Maybe they go on a vacation that he wouldn't have gone on without her, and they're killed in an accident, or any thousands—no millions—of possible variables. Oh, I know it's emotional, but I'm a woman and can't help but worry. They, or at least he, will have to survive in order to bring you home, should you miss the last beam-out. What if that happens? He has her and no motivation. Then he never needs to spend the time on the machine that sent you back there, and we will …"

The more she talked, the more worked up she became.

"*Shhh*, darling, stop. You're worrying for no reason."

With that, she began to softly cry. I just put my arms around her and held her tight. No words would have been appropriate at that moment. I just let her cry it all out. When we reached the hotel, we didn't say much. We just went to bed and acted like a husband and a wife. Later, after she had drifted off to sleep, I stared at the ceiling, thinking about all she had said earlier.

She was right. Because of our romantic involvement, she wasn't just losing her employer and a job; she was losing the man she loved and who loved her. Since falling in love a few years ago, we were more like husband and wife than employer and employee. She had given me everything—her loyalty, love, and her innocence. From previous conversations, I knew that had been a huge step for her and one she had only taken out of love for me. Over the few years, our love had been born and was nurtured and then matured. Frankly, I must admit, I loved being in love.

Occasionally it made me think that it might have been better if I had never discovered where Sheila was when she was killed. Then there would be no reason to return to the past. Not returning would have made Julie happy, yet she said she didn't want to discourage me. This was the first time she had really let it all out.

However, if I didn't go back, what about Doc and Sheila? They would be cheated out of at least forty-three more years of life. His whole life had been spent building a machine to prevent his wife's death. Perhaps I should just go back and tell him it was a dead end and save him from finding out something ugly, like she was having an affair, which was becoming clearer to me as I learned more. Would he really want to know that? Would he still want her back?

That was a step in the right direction. If she was unfaithful, I'd tell him I couldn't find her, and it would remain a huge mystery. At least then Doc could move on. Though I kept forgetting that if I saved her, Doc would forget it all. This time travel stuff was sure confusing at best.

It had started to rain sometime after we arrived back at the hotel, and now it was pouring. The sounds of rain hitting the roof and the occasional rumble of thunder were pleasant to my ears, and sleep came quickly.

The next morning, I got up and peeked out of the window. The sun was shining brightly, and most of the remnants of the rain from the night before, save a puddle or two, were gone. I ordered coffee and muffins from room service and then woke Julie with a kiss on the lips. As I watched her eyes open, loved poured from her gaze. I felt like a king.

"Good morning, beautiful."

She just smiled as she dashed to the bathroom. A knock at the door signaled breakfast had arrived. Right after the deliverer left, she came out. I could see she had washed her face and combed her hair. And as she said good morning and then kissed me, I could tell she had brushed her teeth; I could taste the toothpaste. I chuckled a little as I remembered that she once told me she would never speak to anyone before she brushed her teeth after sleeping.

That morning, we had a better, more positive conversation than we'd had the night before. She was smiling and being her normal witty self again. We were both starting to feel a little amorous when the phone rang. I suggested that they would call back, but I got that look. You know, that look your mom would give you if you didn't do your homework or your chores when she thought they should be done.

My response was simply, "Yes, dear," as I moved to the phone. "Kincannon."

"Yes, Mr. Kincannon. This is Harold Campbell. We spoke yesterday about my brother, John."

"Yes, Mr. Campbell. How are you, sir?"

"I have arranged … I'm fine … a visit with my brother this afternoon at three o'clock. Would that be convenient for you?"

"Yes, that's perfect. Shall we meet you there?"

"Yes. He's at John Hopkins in a special ward paid for by the military, along with several other soldiers. Meet me in the lobby at 2:45. I will introduce you as my son, Corey, who is here on a very short visit from England. I may not be able to get your assistant in, though. I don't want to give them cause to deny us a visit. I hope that's okay with her."

"Oh, that'll be okay. She's riding with me, but she can wait in the lobby."

After we hung up, I went back to where Julie and I had left off. That took us up to the time we had to ready ourselves for the trip. So we had a little lunch, dressed accordingly, and off we went to pick up our rental car and drive to Baltimore.

It was 1430 when we entered John Hopkins. We sat in the lobby to wait for Harold Campbell. The place was large with high ceilings. There was hospital-white paint everywhere, and a flood of people were constantly coming in and out. Nurses by the dozens scurried about like ants foraging for food. An occasional doctor would walk up to the desk, give orders, and then slip away. I didn't see any military people around while we waited.

When Harold walked in about ten minutes later, we spoke briefly. Then he and I went down the hall, turned left, turned right, and then turned left again. It was like walking in a maze. Finally, we reached a set of double doors that led to a nurse's station. There we encountered a nurse who was so tough and straight-faced that she reminded me of a cross between Nurse Mildred Ratched and my senior drill instructor at Parris Island, the marine corps recruit depot. A uniformed army MP was standing there, and an orderly sat with the nurse. Both were very stern-looking guys.

Harold spoke to the nurse. "I'm here to visit my brother, John."

"Yes, Mr. Campbell, and who might this other gentleman be?"

She obviously knew Harold. Now to see if Harold could get his son, Corey—that was me—into see John. At first the nurse refused, but Harold made a passionate plea, and then I added that I had never met my father's only brother, my Uncle Johnny, and because I knew he was up in years, I had traveled a long way for us to know each other. She finally relented.

She had the orderly escort us to John Campbell's room, and then he sat in a chair stationed outside the door. Every door had a chair outside.

Once we were inside the room, Harold introduced me. "Johnny, this is Jake Kincannon, a detective from Chicago trying to get to the bottom of that murder case you witnessed at the Pentagon."

"Hi, John. I doubt they'll give me much time, but it appears that Sheila Wells wasn't kidnapped from the Pentagon parking lot in a black panel truck as you stated at the time of her murder. Can you explain?"

"Harold, is it safe to talk to him?"

Harold nodded.

John looked around like he was about to let me in on a secret. Then he turned to me, saying, "I was given a direct order to say I saw that. I was on duty at the time she was supposed to have been abducted. They brought me in and told me what had happened and what I was to say if questioned, especially by the police and the press. They told me it was a matter of national security. I was young, and I believed them, at least at first. Then I began to think it was wrong, and it dawned on me that by telling them she was kidnapped, I was taking away the chance to capture the real killer. So I went to my superiors and told them it was wrong to withhold information from the police and that I was going to correct my statement. I was immediately arrested on some trumped-up charge of being a spy. Later, they sent me here because they said I had a mental breakdown. I've been here ever since."

"Did you see or know anything of Sheila Wells that you can tell me?"

He just hung his head and shook it. "When I saw her picture in the paper, I realized I had never even seen her around the Pentagon. I didn't think much about that because it's such a large place."

"So, let me be sure I've got this straight. You were told by military officers to tell the story you told because it was vital to national security, and when you wanted to set the record straight, you were arrested to prevent that from happening?"

"Yes, sir. That is exactly what happened."

"Do you remember who gave you this order?"

"I sure do. It was General David Markus, Colonel Thomas Williams, and Captain Bradley Carter. The captain came to me and told me that he was to escort me to General Markus's office immediately. The general told me then, with the others present."

"Did they say why they picked you?"

"I was on duty at that entrance at the approximate time this lady was supposed to have been taken."

"Did they tell you anything about why it was a matter of national security, or anything about the victim?"

Harold sat quietly through all my questioning as though he had heard this story a hundred times. Then he said, "Johnny, Mr. Kincannon is going to try to help you get out of here."

For the first time during our meeting, life came back into John's eyes. A smile swept across his face, and he began to thank me profusely.

"I will do what I can, but I'm only a private investigator. But if we can expose the truth and flush out whoever created this cover-up and why, it should get you out of here."

It was now a little past 1600, and we were told we had to leave. I thanked them for their time and told them I would be in touch. Harold stayed with John, and I left. As I walked back through the maze to the lobby and Julie, I had narrowed it down to two possibilities. Either a powerful individual killed her, someone who could orchestrate the cover-up, or perhaps she had been doing some top-secret stuff that the military didn't want to get out.

I caught up with Julie and filled her in while we walked to the car. We decided to have dinner in Baltimore and then drive back to DC. We found a nice Italian restaurant and had a great meal. Then we talked and speculated about Sheila Wells all the way back to our hotel.

CHAPTER 14

FLORIDA BOUND

First thing the next morning, I was on the phone to Bob Dawson. I told him what I had uncovered and asked if he could locate any of the three officers who had given the orders to John Campbell. I had to interview them. He agreed, and two hours later, after Julie and I returned from breakfast, he had the skinny. It seemed that General Markus died of natural causes twenty-five years ago. Colonel Williams was killed in Vietnam in 1963. However, Captain Bradley Carter had retired six years ago as a one-star general, and was currently living in Fort Lauderdale, Florida. Bob had even gotten me his phone number.

When I told Julie, she said, "I know. Two tickets to Fort Lauderdale on the next available flight."

I just smiled and nodded as I reached for the phone and dialed the number Bob had provided.

"Carter here."

"Good morning, General Carter. My name is Jake Kincannon, and I'm a private investigator looking to clean up a few small details that I think you can help me with. I'll be in Fort Lauderdale tomorrow morning and wondered if I might visit with you for twenty minutes or so."

I was sure I was going to hear him turn me down, in which case I would just show up anyway. However, he seemed more than willing to speak with me. Surprises were always great.

Julie booked our tickets and a room on the beach. By 1500, we were boarding our flight. Three hours later, we were in a cab heading for our room. I had the cabby stop along the way at a telegraph office and sent Doc a note stating our whereabouts and that we were hot on the trail of vital new information. I could have called him from the hotel, but I didn't want to have to answer a lot of potentially uncomfortable questions until I had more information. It was beginning to look more and more like Sheila was involved with another man. I also asked him to send some additional expense money to our hotel in Fort Lauderdale.

When we reached our lodging, we dropped our bags in the room and headed barefoot for the beach. The sun was just beginning to set, and the palm trees were a peaceful sight. The ocean breeze caused their leafy limbs to sway slightly. The slight reddish tint in the few clouds reminded me of an old saying: *Red sky at night, sailors' delight. Red sky in morning, sailors take warning.* I knew the next day would be beautiful.

Julie was a Midwesterner and had never been to an ocean beach. She was thrilled with the sights, the sound of the light surf slapping the shore with each charge and retreat, and the clean, fresh smell of the cool, salty air. She even got to see some bottlenose dolphins swimming by. They seemed so close to shore that it made for an amazing sight.

When we went back to the room, we decided to have a light dinner and relax a bit. Then Julie surprised me when she said, "Let's take a blanket down to the beach." I was up for that.

We waited until we were sure the beach was deserted, and with blankets in tow, we ran down the beach until we found a secluded place between the dunes. It was a fantastic evening, to say the least.

The next morning, we were awakened just before sunup by gulls squawking on the beach. It seemed they were fighting over a fish that had washed ashore during the night. We walked the beach back to our room, had coffee, and then got ready for our noon meeting with the general.

A twenty-minute cab ride with a Jamaican cab driver was most entertaining. He had Bob Marley singing on a cassette tape, and he talked a mile a minute with that great-sounding Jamaican accent. It was already hot, and he drove along without the air-conditioning on and all the windows down. It was still quite entertaining. When we arrived, we found that the general and his wife were most cordial people, not what I expected. Mrs. Carter took Julie for a tour of their home, and the ladies talked and had tea while the general and I went to his study. He closed the door, not so much for privacy but so he could smoke. This was the only place he was allowed to smoke his cigars, and that was with the window open and a fan exhausting the smoke to the outside. He offered me one, and since they were Cuban, I agreed. *Here I go breaking the law. Oh well, some laws don't make sense anyway.*

We had no sooner lit up than in walked his wife with a tray of coffee and light cakes. She was not pleased with two smoke stacks belching out smoke. She seemed to hold her breath, get rid of her cargo, and beat a hasty retreat.

After some small talk about his career, I then asked him, "Sir, do you recall an incident regarding a woman, Sheila Wells, who was raped, beaten, and killed and then dumped into the Potomac River in 1937?"

He didn't react at first, as though the name was unfamiliar to him. And then suddenly his heretofore-congenial face tightened, and he replied, "Who sent you here about that matter?"

I told him we had new evidence that she had not been killed as was reported to police and the newspapers and that a man had been placed in a mental institution because he didn't want to go along with a story he was initially ordered to tell. This on the pretext that her death was a matter of national security.

"I will not confirm any such facts. I have been a military officer most of my life and will not besmirch the service to which I belonged."

"Sir, I am not a reporter, and I have no intention to besmirch anyone or the military. However, the more I dig, the more people that find out, and the worse it gets. This case has been officially reopened by the Arlington County Police, and I know what was done to the young soldier because he wanted to retract his story. I can assure you that if I can find out where Sheila Wells was just prior to her death and if that man at John Hopkins gets released, I will have the case closed, and nothing more will come of it. I know that General Markus was the one who gave the order for the cover-up, and he's dead now. Also, I believe you have enough connections to get John Campbell released."

"John Campbell. Oh my God, we forgot all about him. He was supposed to be kept there until after the war and then court martialed and released. You found he's still there?"

"Yes, he's still there. Get him released and just tell me exactly where Sheila Wells was when she was murdered, and I will never mention this again to a living soul, except my client, her husband."

He seemed to ponder that for a moment or two and then said, "Well, the war has been over for some time, so what can it hurt? I will tell you on one condition and that is that you will never reveal my name, and we never had this conversation. Agreed?"

"You have my word on it, provided you will give me your word that you will get John Campbell out of that retched place he has been in for far too long. Agreed?"

"Yes. I want him released also. That was a grave mistake."

I wanted to ask him to see that John Campbell got an honorable discharge and all the back army pay owed to him, just like he would have received had he been any other serviceman who spent that amount of time in the service of his country. But I knew that would only make my request more difficult, and he might not agree. I wanted it in case my mission to save Sheila ultimately failed, but I knew if I was successful, it would be a moot point anyway because Campbell would never be forced to lie and therefore would never be placed in that situation. It now appears that by saving Sheila, I also give John Campbell his life back. No one would ever know if this change was for the good or not for John personally. Perhaps now instead of being locked away for a large portion of his life, he would get sent off to the battlefield and die. Only John could say which reality would suit him best.

"You have my word as an officer and a gentleman."

We shook on it, and he began. "First, let me tell you that her name, as far as the Germans knew, was Sheila Schmidt. You see, back then I was a young captain and an aide to General Markus. I was also stationed at the Pentagon, and I did know Sheila Wells. She was working as a secretary in the Pentagon until someone discovered that she was fluent in German. When we became concerned that we might end up going to war against Germany, we wanted all the Intel we could garner about them.

"They sent folks down from the CIA to interview, and the CIA, after a thorough interview and training program, decided to use her. She was more than excited about helping her country. It was an operative of the CIA who first approached her and convinced her and excited her, and they planted her in the German embassy. They provided all the proper papers for one Sheila Schmidt, and she became a double agent working for us before WWII, and frankly she was extremely good at it. Very few people knew of her involvement, not even her own husband.

"We knew that a lot of the folks from that embassy hung out socially at the German-American Club on Fifteenth Street. After awhile, it seemed to be populated more and more by people sympathetic to Hitler and his politics. So she was told to hang out there and, when the opportunity arose, to denounce this country. She was also told to let it be known to anyone interested that she worked at the Pentagon.

"It wasn't long before an aide to the German ambassador approached her, one Hans Steckel. Rumor was that she became the lover of this aide to the ambassador, feeding him phony information while gleaning good intel for our side. She worked directly for the CIA, and General Markus was the military liaison. The CIA told us only what we needed to know, so I didn't know her whereabouts most of the time or on the night of her death. The CIA called General Markus at his home very early on the morning of her death and told him how to handle it. When I next saw the general, he told me to find someone who could have seen her that night and feed everyone the story that Mrs. Wells was abducted by a person or persons unknown in a black Ford panel truck. That way, it would appear to just be some sexual deviant that would get away, and eventually the case would grow cold as the nation focused on the war. I checked the duty roster and found that Corporal John Campbell was on duty at the west entrance the night before. I ordered him to see General Markus."

"Who was the contact at the CIA?"

"At that time, the only name I ever heard the general talk about was Dennis Webster. I came to know him again after I made colonel. We worked another operation together."

"Would you know or connect me with someone who might know his whereabouts?"

"Yes, I do. He is also retired and lives in West Palm Beach, Florida. We play golf together occasionally. But you could end up dead if you tried to approach him yourself about a matter like this. Let me see what I can do."

He stood, walked to the phone, and dialed it. I could only hear his side of the conversation.

"Denny, it's Brad Carter. Yes, I know it's been awhile. You need to get down here and let's play some golf. What? Oh no, not likely.

"Say, listen, Denny. The reason I called is I want to search your memory banks. Yeah." The general chuckled. "Mine too, but I was trying to remember the name of the woman who you had planted in the German embassy just prior to us entering the war with Germany. The attractive blonde that you and General Markus recruited."

There was a rather lengthy pause. Then the conversation continued.

"Who? Oh yes, that's it. Sheila Schmidt. Say, I always meant to ask you, where and when was she was killed? What? No, I'm not writing my memoirs. I just got to thinking about her and wondered. You know me. It drives me crazy when I can't recall something.

"Really? Are you sure? Yes, and she was in the Mayflower Hotel on that night? Really? How interesting. With whom was she with there?"

There was another even longer silence from the general, as if he was receiving a lot of data. I was hoping for that and hoping the CIA guy would give up all the details.

Finally, the general responded, "I always remembered that she was such a handsome woman, although I only saw her a couple of times. What's that? Oh no, I'm a happily married man. When? Yes, I'll be in town then, and you can stay with us. Okay. I'm looking forward to it. I always enjoyed spanking you in a round of golf and would love to do so again. Not on your best day, my friend. Sure, just be sure to bring money because I don't take IOUs! Okay, you're on. See you then, and thanks for the refresher. Good-bye."

He hung up the phone, walked back to his chair, sat down, and said, "Well, according to my CIA friend, they—the CIA—followed her to the Pentagon visitor parking lot where she was picked up and transported to the Mayflower Hotel. She was to be picked up by limo and delivered there, where she was to meet up with one Hans Steckel. I knew he was an aide, but according to Webster, he was also an SS officer. She was followed there approximately two to three times a week. She was open with Dennis about the fact that she used her feminine ways to get him to give up sensitive info while feeding him bogus intel. She said pillow talk was most informative. Webster said she was more a spy than some of the trained operatives with the company. Both what she gleaned and what she fed them helped us know a lot about what the Nazis were planning. We were able to get some info to our allies and saved many lives.

"She also confided in Webster that her husband didn't know of her clandestine activities and that if anything happened to her, he was not to know. Her husband only knew his wife worked for the Pentagon; that was all. She was savvy enough to know it would be too dangerous for both of them if he knew. Besides, Sheila told Webster that her husband was quite self-absorbed, so it was easy to keep this a secret from him. Webster told me that he even made a play for her, but she turned him down cold. She told him what she did was for the country and that she loved her husband dearly."

I was thrilled to hear that part most of all, and I felt relieved and happy for Doc, but he could never know what she had really been doing. I had a plan already worked out in my mind as to what I would tell Doc if I was successful in rescuing her. Sheila and I would have to work out a clear understanding of the facts of how I saved her from the man in the black panel truck. Then no one but Sheila or me could disprove this new "official story."

The general continued, "Webster knew the routine was that she left home every day as though she was going to her job at the Pentagon, and she did park her car there. She would then be picked up by a man in plain clothes, usually driving a limo but not always, and taken to the German embassy. Presumably, the man was another person from the embassy. There she worked as a secretary of the aide to the ambassador."

"Excuse me, General, but how could she work at the embassy and still get kidnapped from the Pentagon parking lot?"

"That was the interesting part. Once Sheila was recruited as a double agent, her role as such worked extremely well. You see, as an employee at the Pentagon, her car, like those of all personnel who worked or were assigned there, military or civilian, had a parking pass glued to the car's front bumper. No sticker, you couldn't get through the gates. Also, should a car be found without a sticker in the personnel parking lots, it would be searched and impounded. She would arrive at the Pentagon on Mondays, Wednesdays, and Fridays and walk to where someone from the German embassy picked her up. On Tuesdays, Thursdays, and Saturdays, she would be in her office at the Pentagon as usual. Those in the know on both sides knew of this and covered for her when she was missing from either place. The Germans thought that on her days at the Pentagon, she was gathering intel for them, and the Americans knew that when she was at the embassy, she was gathering intel for our side."

"Oh, that is quite interesting." I thought, *That's why she asked to meet me at the Pentagon on Saturday when I spoke with her by phone.*

"I understand that the CIA gave her full discretion to do whatever was necessary to obtain the information. Then one morning when I reported for work, the general was already there, and that was highly unusual. In fact, it had never happened in all the time I worked for him, except that one day. He called me into his office and told me she had been kidnapped and to find him a witness. That, as you know, was Campbell.

"Webster said the speculation was that German Intelligence must have discovered her role as a spy. They decided to keep her and feed her only what they wanted the Americans to know, thus making her an unwilling accomplice in their endeavors. When the intel was determined to be bogus, we were ordered to pull her out. Unfortunately, we were too late."

Carter told me Sheila's affair with the aide to the ambassador lasted for about six months. During most of that time, she was very effective and able to get useful information on what the Germans were really doing. But eventually they apparently got on to her. So, day by day, German Intelligence began feeding her garbage, and by night she sweet-talked the info out of Hans. Hans was a little man, and not very attractive, but he had an ego the size of Texas, and more importantly, he knew everything the ambassador knew. When she showed Hans a little interest, he bit like a hungry catfish, and Sheila skillfully reeled him in, into bed, and out of information vital to the Americans and their allies. Webster debriefed her daily, and at one point she mentioned that her husband was getting sick of all the "overtime" she had been pulling lately. Hans, on the other hand, was lapping up the attention and the sex and had a certain smugness about the fact that he was taking the fruit from some American slob's wife.

History had recorded Sheila's death on May 11, 1937. Her body had washed up on the Arlington County, Virginia, side of the Potomac River later that morning, raped, badly beaten, and floating face down near the shore. A man fishing from a small boat found her nude body at 0730. The coroner's office estimated the time of death as between midnight and 0200. The police investigated, got Campbell's statement, and quickly wrote it off as a sex crime, and of course, a killer was never caught. The CIA knew exactly what had happened and to whose hands her death was really attributable. However, they could never do or say anything about what they knew without letting the Germans and the public know—both of which could, in the military's opinion, have hurt the war effort. To this day, Doc believed what the police told him, and why shouldn't he? He would never know differently from me.

Carter went on to explain, "What had really happened that night was that earlier that day, German Intelligence had discovered the secret affair between Sheila and Hans, and they informed him of what they knew. We felt that was when he plotted her demise. Unfortunately, we pieced that together after the fact. The military coroner stated in his report that they used a bayonet from an American-made M1 rifle to finish her. The blade had been fully imbedded in her chest, and it was still in her heart when they recovered the body. She had been tortured to the point that death must have been a relief. Her nipples had been cut off, and her face and body were badly bruised and cut with hundreds of little slices not more than an inch in length, not enough to kill but enough to cause intense pain.

"Hans must have had the room cleaned and then disposed of the body. No police report existed of a killing in that hotel on that date. With that, the book was closed on the CIA operative named Sheila Schmidt. The CIA would disavowal her ever working for them or knowing anything about her if ever queried."

Now that I was armed with the facts of what had really happened surrounding Sheila's death, I could put together a plan to save her. I thanked my host and reminded him of his promise regarding John Campbell. Then Julie and I said our farewells. We could now fly back to Chicago and tell Doc what we had discovered, with the exception of the spying and affair with Hans, no matter how noble it may have been. I now knew exactly how I would describe to Doc what actually happened to Sheila and how I would save her. Now to get back to home, make my final trip to and from 1937, and stop all the time jumping. It was a most satisfying feeling. Little did I know at that moment what loomed in my future!

CHAPTER 15

UNINTENDED CONSEQUENCES

We caught the next flight back to Chicago. By the time we got home, there was nothing to do but sleep. Well, almost nothing.

Bright and early the next morning, I was at Doc's door. "Good morning, Doc. I have good news!"

"Come in, my boy. I have coffee on. Tell me. Don't just stand there gaping at me."

We walked toward his office, and he grabbed me a cup of coffee on the way.

"Okay, Doc, here's the skinny. Everything happened just as we read in the paper, and you remember—"

"Can't be!" The look of disappointment on his face was pathetic.

"Now hold on, Doc. Stop interrupting me. As I said, everything was the same except for one tiny little detail. It was the north entrance, not the west entrance! Now that I know exactly where she was on that fateful night, the answer is simple. I'll simply go back in time to just before I left her on my last trip, which was 1600, and stay with her until 0130. You have to simply make the coordinates for my extraction at the house you lived in at that time. And I need to stay with her until the last possible moment. Simple, right?"

"Genius, my boy. Sheer genius."

"Can you beam me back to exactly 1530 to your front door coordinates?"

"You bet I can."

"Then I'll still be there with Sheila, and history will pick up where I left off, but instead of leaving at 1600 as I did on the first trip, I'll stay

105

until approximately one hour before her original death. Then there can be no reason whatsoever for her to backtrack to the Pentagon parking lot, regardless of the entrance."

"Yes, quite right. And yes, that is possible. But there's still one thing. Why did she return to the Pentagon after you left the last time?"

He caught me a bit flat-footed on that one, so I just said she had forgotten a report that was due the next day and was not quite finished. He seemed to buy it.

He started rubbing his hands together and said, "Are you prepared to go back right now?"

I thought for a second and then said, "Sure, why not? Let's get it done."

I changed into my period-correct clothes, restocked my supply of old money, and stepped into the pod. In an instant, I was standing there with Sheila.

"Let me get your hat. I know you said you had to leave at four."

"It seems that won't be necessary now. I can and have to stay here with you until just before midnight."

"Really! And why is that?"

"Because I have to prevent you from going to meet Hans Steckel." The look that came over her face was one I wished I could record; it was one of sheer terror, like her husband had caught her with him in bed.

"Does Will know?" She seemed more concerned about what Doc knew than for her life.

"Oh, don't worry. Doc knows nothing of this, and he won't unless you tell him, which I strongly recommend you *not* do."

Her facial expression changed immediately, and she breathed a heavy sigh. A partial smile returned. I told her the whole story I had learned, and she was more than happy to have me stay. She then informed me that Steckel knew where she lived and that we just needed to be sure they didn't come for her at the house. Now she was scared. We talked, she fixed me dinner, and we listened to the radio until it was time for me to leave. I walked to the foyer, and I was gone, back to my time in 1980. I had no idea what shocking reality would be waiting for me.

When I looked through the porthole in the pod, I saw Doc, but it was a strange and concerning sight. He had a huge scar across the side of his face from his temple to his chin, but it was an old scar. How could that be? I left him but minutes ago in his time. The door popped open, and he was all aflutter.

"Jake, sit down quickly. We did something wrong, and I figured it out while you were gone."

I was frozen with dread. "Doc, where's Sheila?"

"She's not here, Jake!"

"What the hell happened?"

"Sit down and listen. You saved Sheila. I had her with me for an additional ten years, until she was arrested as an enemy of the state, tried, and found guilty and sentenced to life in prison. She is in prison and has been since 1947 after a man named Hans Steckel became the chancellor of West Germany in 1946."

I would soon find out that this West Germany was not the same West Germany that I read about in school after WWII and I knew as half the country of Germany. According to the history I had known, there was even a wall built in 1961 to separate the democratic western half of Germany from the Russian-controlled eastern half of Germany. The wall was known as the Berlin Wall, and it split the capital city nearly in half. No, this West Germany was the eastern half of the United States of America!

"Jake, to get you back here, Sheila told me about the Teleporter and the trunks, but I didn't believe her. In order to convince and motivate me, she told me everything about Hans Steckel and her spying and even her affair with him to garner German intel. It took her telling me everything to anger me enough to find the trunk. That's how I know, so you don't need to waltz around it, Jake. She even told me that when you were with her when last I sent you back how you promised not to tell me." So Doc knew why Steckel had her arrested. Things were beginning to make sense about this new reality. I let Doc continue the history he had lived with since I saved Sheila.

"Funny thing, Jake, this Steckel fellow was the one who ordered her arrest. Yet when the jury found her guilty and sentenced her to hang, he stepped in and commuted her sentence to life in prison. There is not much time. You must go back right away, and God only knows what horrors she must have endured there in that prison."

I had my doubts that she was enduring much hardship. Even though Doc knew everything, he didn't think Hans would enjoy her after she was sent to prison. She was likely saving her skin by playing nice with Hans, knowing I would return and change it all again, or at least hoping I would. Doc went on to tell me the highlights of his history. Fortunately, he was able to gather the raw materials to build it before the war was lost. So, here I was, back in my time, 1980, to find in my horror the new world order. Doc told me the details of how it happened. America went to war with Japan and then Germany, just as history recorded, but something radically changed. Hitler was assassinated on October 5, 1939, and Hermann Goering took over as chancellor and supreme commander of the Nazi forces. He was a military man and knew how to wage war. With Goering at the helm, he didn't make the mistake Hitler made to invade Russia in the dead of winter. Instead, he signed a treaty with them, one they both honored.

Goering promised to give Russia the countries of Norway, Sweden, and Finland as a reward for staying out of the war or joining them in their conquest for global dominance. With nothing to fear from the Russians, he hit Great Britain with everything he had until Churchill had to surrender. With one of our best allies out of the war, Goering turned his attention to us. He knew we were the only force that could cost him the war, but he also knew our attentions were divided. He believed that we were now at our most vulnerable point, so he then turned all his available forces on us. He put his submarines, called U-boats, along the East Coast, looking only to sink troop and supply ships.

Goering set up a naval blockade to take out anything that got past the subs. Then he sent bombers over the top from Greenland to bomb the major cities along the East Coast. He was too smart to send troops into the United States. He just pummeled us as he had done to England, with airpower. We were forced to pull back our troops out of Europe and the Pacific islands and protect our flanks. The thinking was that we would not lose troops and supplies moving them within our borders, and we could get them on the East or West Coasts relatively quickly when needed. We even tried sending fresh troops and supplies to aid in the war in Europe and sent them around the West Coast, which took much longer and grounded our troops in Europe.

Mexico and Canada fought alongside us. When Mexico fell, we had to put more troops against that border. Then Canada fell a year later. We were now exposed by two great landmasses. No longer did our enemies have to fight from ships. They could refuel their planes from Mexico, Canada, and even Cuba.

"Without troops and ships to fight the Japanese in the Pacific, they hopscotched from island to island until they took all the Pacific Islands, including the Philippines and Hawaii. We were fighting the Germans on the East Coast and then the Japanese on the West Coast. It was as though we were being eaten from both ends. Goering sent an ambassador to see the president and told him of their discovery of a bomb, already in production, so powerful it could wipe out entire cities and leave massive amounts of radiation that would kill thousands of people. Since we were also working on such a bomb, Roosevelt knew how destructive it would be. Roosevelt panicked and surrendered under threat of that atomic bomb, which Germany had beaten us to the punch in building. They split the country into two countries. Germany has everything east of the Rockies, and Japan has the rest, plus all the Pacific islands."

Doc went on to explain that the country was still a very tough place for anybody German or Japanese. The second amendment put weapons in every American's hands for this very purpose. Our forefathers worried about just such an occasion when they wrote it into the Constitution. That coupled with the enormity of this country had thousands of militia groups hid in mountains, valleys, and wooded areas out of sight of the enemy. They killed anyone wearing a police or military uniform. Now our sons, as soon as they were big enough to hold a weapon, fought these monstrous invaders. They beat us on paper, but the tough American citizens fought on. It was rumored that no German, Japanese, or their allies wanted to pull duty in the old USA for this very reason. Seems you have to be beaten to find the courage to fight to the death for what you believe in. The hippies of the seventies—yeah, the make love not war crowd—were now gun-toting purveyors of death. Although they never became the hippies, as I knew from the Viet Nam War … there was no Viet Nam War or Korean War either. Yet, according to Doc, many more people died under these dictators than ever died in the Korean or Viet Nam Wars combined.

Doc even showed me the map of the world as it was now. I stood there in shock and disbelief as I viewed the map. There it was, a jagged line cutting the western portion of the United States along the Rocky Mountains from Canada to Mexico. The eastern half was labeled West Germany, just as Doc had stated. Russia remained as it was before with the addition of the Norwegian countries Goering had promised. All the eastern European countries, like Poland, France, and the British Isles, to name a few, were now called Germany, and the countries that no longer existed were like states in the old United States. I couldn't believe what I was seeing. West of the Rockies was called simply Territory of Japan. It sent chills down my spine.

"After we surrendered, Hans Steckel became chancellor of West Germany—a reward for his courage in masterminding the killing of Hitler. He even bragged about it, said Hitler would have cost them the war. Goering himself appointed Steckel in 1946 before Goering died of heart disease in 1950." All that Doc told me was now recorded history.

"So, Doc, what this amounts to is that I have single-handedly turned turned the world into one that is dominated by ruthless dictators?" That was not the history I knew; we won the war in my history. Doc was right; I had to go back right away. I couldn't afford to get caught there by them, or history would never be changed.

Chapter 16

My Last Hurrah

We had to make a new plan, and quickly. I had to go back and save Sheila again, but now I also had to kill Steckel. We thrashed out how it must be done. It was agreed that I would go back to the exact time and date of my first trip. It would be a fresh start to clean up any slight mistake that could have altered history, other than that which we wished to alter. I would not meet the younger Doc or his wife this time. Limit my contact with everyone as much as possible. Then find a way into the room at the Mayflower before Hans got into bed with her and kill him and escape with her and send her back home to Doc—and to live. That was great on paper, but could I pull it off? I had to. The world as I knew it depended on it.

"Doc, we have a good plan. Send me back. I'm ready."

I stood up, ready to go back. Doc stood, put his hand on my shoulder, and hung his head.

"There is only one problem that I must tell you about."

I turned and headed toward the pod. "Come on, Doc. We're wasting time. I must get back and stop him!"

Doc didn't move. He just blurted out, "You'll never come home!"

I stopped dead in my tracks and turned around to face him. "What the hell do you mean by that?"

"There's only enough fuel to get you back to 1937, but not enough to get you back home, I'm sorry to say."

I sat back down hard and began to think, first selfishly and then more realistically. I fought against it, but there was really no choice. There was no time to find and bring a braver man than me up to speed. Doc couldn't do it. He wasn't able to handle a man like Steckel. Yes, there was only me. I had to go back. There was really no choice; I was the only man that could. I wasn't thinking about being an unknown hero. I just couldn't stand

111

the thought of my country that I loved so much being run by dictators. Suddenly this wasn't just about saving one woman; it was now about saving the world from cruel and evil dictators. I had no choice, no choice at all. We were a free nation, and it had to stay that way. I would have to be very careful living out my years in the past and hope that Doc would find a way to get fuel to bring me back.

It was logical. I had to hold on to that thought. So I swallowed hard, took a deep breath, and stood again. "That's okay, Doc. It will be worth it, and if I'm successful, you'll know it. Sheila will be here, and the world will be safe. I'll have Sheila tell you all that's happened with the changes. She'll know all about Julie and you, and she must take care of her for me. When she returns, and America is safe again, you'll know that means I'm okay, and I'll make my life there. I'll ask her to see that you keep trying to get more fuel and retrieve me."

"I will, Jake. I promise you I will, and when I can bring you back you will come back on this date and not have aged a bit."

There was no time to see Julie, and furthermore, another good-bye would just worsen the situation or even make me change my mind. I had to get back there and accept my awesome responsibility.

Doc and I shook hands and then hugged. We didn't speak of it, but it seemed obvious that we were both thinking we might never see each other again. Then Doc dialed me into an area near the Mayflower Hotel. There I would get a room and devise the minute details of my plan to save Sheila and, even more importantly, how to kill Hans Steckel. I stood inside the pod, staring at a sad-looking Doc as the machine began its whirring sound. We waved to each other, and I was gone, back to the past and a major history-changing event. It was hard to believe that one man could set off a chain of events that could so change the world.

I materialized in the alley behind the Mayflower Hotel and made note of my exact location for retrieval purposes, whenever they might come and walked around to the front, and got a room. Doc had sent me back to the time I had arrived on my first trip, May 7, 1937. That was necessary to erase everything I had done on my trips before, to sterilize it, if you will. Oh, I would still remember each trip and what did or didn't happen. All this would be forever in my brain. I wondered if successful, would the undone memories eventually fade away as the nonreality that they would have rendered? As I thought of that, I chuckled. Knowing those past trips, I would *not* get involved with Crystal this time, and even though it happened, it would only be in my memory because in the new reality, it just didn't happen. But I would not see Julie again for a long time, forty-three years to be exact, or maybe never. It also meant I had to do my time in the past and stay away from as many people as possible so as not to effect the future in some way, tampering with history in some other way that could lead to some other unknown consequence in the future. Doc had given me plenty of money, which was no longer good in the time I had just left. German Marks were the currency now. I paid for the room from May 7 through May 11.

I no longer had the luxury of failing. I couldn't just step on the beam point and try again. This was it—curtains up and no more dress rehearsals. No more rescues, no more chances to do it again.

Another reality rattled my consciousness. *If I save Sheila, I must also kill Hans. If I don't save Sheila, I must let Hans live.* Whatever the subtle change was in killing her in the hotel versus killing her in her own home, it had to be left alone. I could not let her die at home. If I didn't get it right, the world would become a very dark place. So obviously I would not interact with her, as that may have been the problem. I would kill Hans or she would have to die in the hotel.

I would have never guessed that one day I would carry such an awesome responsibility or that one man, Hans Steckel, could change the course of history so dramatically. Imagine, the fate of the free world rested in the hands of Jake Kincannon and whether or not I would be successful in taking another life in order to save it. I would most likely have to go to a war that I had only read about, and whether Steckel lived or died would determine if my life would help save the world or cast it into total domination by evil men.

I prayed over and over for God to aid me in my quest and to forgive me for asking for it. I would have several days to contemplate this thought, how I would do it, and Julie. What would become of Julie, whether I was successful or not? Then there was my life, trapped in a strange time. I guessed it would be bad for me if I failed and unknown if I succeeded. Things sure had taken a turn. Today was the day on my first trip when I first spoke with Sheila. On this trip, we would not speak until the final moment of truth, whatever truth that would turn out to be. My brain churned through thoughts of all this and more until I resorted to several belts from Mr. Jack Daniels to put me to sleep.

On day two, I slipped across the street for a quick breakfast, trying to draw as little attention to myself as possible. Afterward, I stopped at the newsstand next door to the diner and bought several books to read. There I saw a leather-bound journal and bought it to record my time here. I wasn't sure why; it just struck me as a good idea, as well as another way to deal with the long hours until rescue time. I paid for my treasures and scurried back to my room. I was really paranoid about somehow doing something else that would have devastating effects on the future.

I sat down and wrote out all I could remember from the time I first met Doc until now, recording the dates to the best of my recollection. I planned to sleep, write, read, and listen to the radio. As each day passed, the old history I had created from previous trips here was erased, returning it to the history before Doc and I changed it. Sheila would not have any advance warning like she had when I came before. Because of this, I had no way to know what she would do or whether she would believe this fantastic story or not. Perhaps she would try to save Steckel. Sheila, the person I was sent to save, was now a variable, and she could unwittingly become the instrument of my death. What would happen to history if that happened? I could not let that happen. I couldn't try to warn her ahead of time because she might do something unexpected and change something I couldn't fix. Again, there would be no second chances. I had to take my chances with her and hope. I had to kill Steckel, even if it cost Sheila and me our lives, but even that I couldn't be sure of. I was really on the horns of a dilemma. My safest bet was to hide out until the last minute and get into that hotel room and kill him, no matter what else happened. My hope was that I could, kill him, save her, get safely away from there, and then start a new life, as strange as that sounded.

The next few days slowly slipped by, and it was now May 10, 1937. Tonight Sheila would meet Hans in their usual room, 313 of the Mayflower Hotel, and Hans would feed her champagne and a light supper, take her one last time, and then turn her over to his goon squad to rape, sodomize, and torture her, which would ultimately culminate in her death. But somewhere between the champagne and her undressing, I would arrive. I would swiftly kill him and remove her from room 313 to a cab, taking her back to the Pentagon parking lot and sending her home to Doc.

I walked across the street to the diner and ordered steak and eggs, a traditional marine corps breakfast before going into battle. By 0200 tomorrow, Nazis and Japs would rule the future world or it would be as I knew it before Doc and I teamed up. I would do everything within my power to see it is the latter. After my meal, I returned to my room and waited for the moment when I would start Operation Rescue, as I decided to call it.

CHAPTER 17

MISSION IMPOSSIBLE

From what I knew of what happened that night, Sheila would arrive around 1900. Hans would be waiting and had ordered champagne and a light dinner as soon as she arrived. I remembered that from the CIA surveillance info I got from General Carter, that at 1730, Hans would receive a call to confirm her arrival and be told that three SS operatives would arrive at 2100 and do what they had to do. Hans, of course, had built in enough time to have sex with her one last time, and then when the three Nazi SS troopers came in, they would rape and sodomize her before killing her in a slow, brutal fashion. Only, I had a different idea.

I was dressed in my disguise and waiting in the elevator lobby of the third floor by 1915 hours. Hans and Sheila were both in the room. There I waited for room service for room 313. Within ten minutes, the elevator door opened, and the bellboy pushing a cart that held champagne and two plates of food followed a man who exited onto that floor. The man turned to the left hallway, and the bellboy turned to the right toward room 313. "Young man?"

He stopped and looked at me, seemingly puzzled by my dress. "Yes, sir?"

"Are you taking that food to room 313?"

"Yes, sir."

"Say, listen, the couple staying in that room are dear old friends of mine, and I would like to play a little joke on them—surprise them, you see? Here's ten dollars for you if you let me deliver the food to them. What do you say?"

"Well, I don't—"

"How about twenty dollars?" I interrupted.

"Well, I guess it would be okay."

"Here's the twenty and five more for keeping this between you and me. Okay?"

"Yes, sir. Thank you, sir!"

"Now remember, this is our secret."

"Yes, sir. Mum's the word!"

The young lad retreated to the elevator. He would never learn of his participation in the events that were about to take place. I pushed the cart to the room and knocked. When the door opened, there stood Hans. At last I was face to face with the man who had some part in turning the world upside down. I would likely never know all the details and how it would play out so differently simply because a murder that took place in a different time was altered by saving that life and exchanging it for another. When I saw him, I was filled with hatred, first because he was a part of the Nazi war machine that had conquered the world and second because he had caused the heinous death of Doc's wife.

Since I was finally in the right place at the right time, I was hopefully going to change history forever, and killing him would be an easy thing for me to do. One less Nazi had to be a good thing. I had a switchblade knife in my pocket and a snubbed-nose thirty-eight in a holster under my arm. However, I hoped to kill him with my bare hands. There would be less blood and noise that way.

"Boy, just put the cart over there," he said, and handed me a fifty-cent piece.

I couldn't help but think this coin would be worth about twenty bucks in my time. I did as he said, and then I heard Sheila call from the bedroom. I knew her voice all too well from previous visits. But that was all erased for her as I changed history by starting this trip back at day one of my first trip, not giving her advance notice as in the past trips. That meant she had no clue who or what I was. Her reaction to what would happen was the unknown factor.

"Hans, is that the—" She stopped when she came into the room and saw me. "Oh, I didn't realize the bellboy was still here." She quickly turned and walked back into the bedroom.

"Hurry up, boy. Can't you see I have a guest?"

"Yes, sir."

I set the cart where he instructed and walked past him, heading for the door. As I passed him, he turned to the bedroom. I turned sharply, threw my right hand around his head, and snapped the side of my flattened palm back into his throat as hard as I could, rendering him unable to scream or even speak. At the same time, I struck down hard on his butt with my left hand, causing him to fall backward. Then I slipped my left hand over his shoulder, clasped my hands together, and tightened it while pulling his head into my shoulder and stepping backward.

It takes longer to describe the technique than to do it. This was a simple method for taking a sentry from the rear so he couldn't yell out. I was taught this simple but very effective technique in the marine corps. Fifteen seconds to unconsciousness, and thirty seconds to death. At first he kicked to try to free himself, but within seconds he was just convulsing and then nothing. I held it even longer to be sure.

Meanwhile, Sheila heard nothing. After he went limp, I checked his carotid artery for a pulse. There was none. He was dead all right. My time in the marines had taught me well. That was the end of Hans. Hopefully, that put history back to how it was, and a divided Germany would be the result of the ending of the war in Europe. Now I had to get her dressed and out of there. Could I pull this off and accomplish the original mission?

Next, I went into the bedroom and snuck up behind her. When she turned, I clasped my hand over her mouth and quickly said, "You must be quiet. I have to get you out of here quickly. Your life depends on it. I have been sent by Dennis Webster." I already had a story made up that was more believable than the truth.

She had terror in her eyes, so I spoke softly and clearly to her. "My name is Jake Kincannon, and I'm with army intelligence. Your cover has been blown, and three undercover SS officers are on their way here to kill you and dispose of your body. Promise not to scream, and I'll let go. Okay?"

She looked deeply into my eyes, like she was trying to see if I was telling the truth. I maintained eye contact with her until she nodded. Now came the moment of truth. I knew there were guards for Steckel not far away. If she screamed, it would surely bring them down on us. I slowly released my grip.

"Sheila, German Intelligence has discovered your little fling with Hans and that you're a double agent. They told him yesterday and instructed him as to what to do with you. Now please get dressed quickly. I have to get you to my room quickly, and after I give you all the information for your safe relocation, I will get you to a cab and back to your car in the Pentagon parking lot. Move quickly!"

She nodded and ran to the bathroom and dressed while I wiped down the place for prints. I wasn't sure why I did that, knowing my prints wouldn't exist for many years. Just caution, I guess.

We walked out to the elevator, apparently unseen, and took it up to my room. Once inside, I sat her on the couch and poured her a stiff bourbon.

"Sheila, you must pay close attention to what I'm about to tell you. Okay?"

Her hands trembling, she took a healthy sip and nodded. Then I told her the rest of my concocted story.

"You must take the cab I will get you to shortly and go straight to your car and then straight home. Okay?"

She couldn't speak, so she just nodded again. I noticed a tear run down her left cheek, but she made not a sound. I had to tell her everything and that she had to have Will, as she referred to Doc, retrieve one of those two trunks.

I told her I was from the future and that in forty-three years I must be retrieved. I told her about the fuel situation that left me there. I told her that I had been sent back to save her life by her husband. I told her that there would be a Julie Carson, who wouldn't know me but that we had a life together that started as her working for me. I gave her a copy of what had been left for Julie, without the part Julie wrote for herself.

"As you know, your husband recently inherited some money and real estate in Chicago when his father passed. He has wanted to relocate there, and you even asked your supervisor about a transfer to the Chicago office, and she told you that you could have it. Tomorrow, you will tell her that you will accept that Chicago position after all. He will get his doctorate from DePaul University. But this is the critical part: you must *never* reveal that any of this ever happened—your spying, your affair, nothing. That's my present to Doc. You will come home tonight like every other night, and your life and Doc's life will be whatever you two make it, and I hope you will be happy. You have no idea how much Doc has sacrificed for you. You'll just have to trust me on that one."

Then she looked up and spoke for the first time. "Why do you keep calling him Doc?"

"Because after you get to Chicago, he will return to school and get his PhD. It was much later that I met him as a result of him calling my detective agency, and he enticed me to take the job, and here I am. Remember to tell Doc to go to the attic of his father's house and retrieve the chest that he will find there and then do whatever it takes to find me and bring me home. I will go to the coordinates as we planned; it's all in my notes here in this envelope. You may be thinking I'm crazy, but please, just see that Doc retrieves the trunk and goes through it thoroughly. Again, my name is Jake Kincannon, private investigator. If you promise me that, I will see you again. Oh, and by the way, I still want that cherry kuchen."

"But I don't understand … this is just so unbelievable."

"Believe me, I understand, but it's getting late. Do you think you're okay? Do you think you're steady enough to drive home?"

"Yes, I think so. Jake Kincannon, I owe you my life."

"Just be safe and see that Doc gets me home."

I walked her to the elevator and then led her to a cab outside the hotel. We talked a little more as we rode to the Pentagon visitor's parking lot. Her car was the only one there. I had the cab wait while I walked her to her car. Once she was behind the wheel and the car was started, I kissed her cheek and told her I would see her again, if she made sure Doc did as he promised me in the future—in the old, unrevised future, that is.

My job was now complete and, thankfully, successful on both counts. I stood and watched her drive away, knowing all that I knew. Everything I wanted was waiting across the sea of time. I thought I would go to the bar and have a drink; hell, I might even get drunk. I didn't have anything better to do for the next forty-three years. I hopped back into the cab and asked where one might get a drink, preferably some all-night joint. He told me of a bar in Virginia. It wasn't close, but hell, I had no place to go anyway.

It was a joint at a place known as Bailey's Crossroads, an out-in-the-country place. He told me all about it, and I figured maybe he had spent some time there. I watched out the rear window for signs of anyone following and didn't see anyone. Thank goodness for that. I'd had all the excitement I could stand for one day. It was not very often that I got to save a beautiful woman and the world all in one day! I now knew how Superman must have felt.

I walked into the bar and found it was a private club, so I paid the twenty-five dollars and became a member. I sat down at a corner table and ordered a double Jack on the rocks. I barely had two sips when in walked two goons. They seemed out of place, and I wondered if they were some of Hans's men after me. How could they be? My actions in room 313 went better than I had expected. No one saw me … did they? They looked around, and I wasn't sure if they saw me or not, but they sat at the end of the bar closest to the door. My mind jumped back and forth from *they couldn't possibly be after me* to *they're here to kill me*. These clowns were ruining my already crazy day.

I asked the waitress if there was a back door, and she said yes but that it was for deliveries and was now locked. One of the men kept looking over his shoulder in my direction. My imagination was getting the better of me, and my suspicions began to grow that they were waiting for me to leave so they could kill or capture me outside. Neither option was acceptable, but how did I get out of there? I casually finished my drink, put on my hat, tipped it down over my eyes, and tried to walk out unnoticed. Not tonight. They followed me, and when I hit the street, I began running as fast as I could in an attempt to shake them, but I felt a stinging sensation alongside my head. That was the last thing I remembered.

Chapter 18

Something's Wrong

That was the last thing I remembered, that is until I woke up in a hospital bed. When I first opened my eyes, everything was a blur. I could see a closed door and a stand to the left of the door with a picture of some kind above it. I could feel something in my arm. I closed my eyes again and was about to drift into sleep when I heard a voice.

"Good morning, sir." It was the voice of an angel.

When I opened my eyes, I saw a woman dressed in white, but still my vision was blurred, and I couldn't make out her features. I tried to rub my eyes, but there was a bandage where my left eye used to be, and as I felt around, I found that it was also covering my forehead and the top of my head as well.

I heard that soft voice again. "Good morning. Glad you are back with us. Sir, do you know who and where you are?" Her voice was calm and pleasing to the ear.

"Well, of course I know who I am. I'm ..." I thought for a second. "I'm Richard Nixon, and it appears I'm in a hospital." It was the first name that came to mind. Besides, no one would look at me funny. It would be a good while before he would become vice president and later president.

"Mr. Nixon, you had no identification on you, so we had no way to know. I will change your chart from John Doe to Richard Nixon." She said my name slowly as she wrote it on the chart. "Do you remember what happened to you?"

I struggled with the bits and pieces rolling around in my head, looking for a slot to fit them into so I could make sense of this. Finally, it began to coalesce in my consciousness.

"Yes, I remember. Two guys were chasing me, trying to rob me, I suspect. Then I felt something hit my head, and then I heard your voice." I couldn't get found out. They couldn't know that I didn't exist, and I couldn't have the Nazis find me.

"Yes, you were found unconscious in the alley behind a bar in Bailey's Crossroads. The police just happened to be parked across the street and saw them chasing you. You're lucky they were there. The men got away, but that probably saved your life. You were shot in the head, but again lucky, as it was a glancing wound. You weren't totally lucky, because they got away with your wallet. You have been our guest here ever since." Perhaps it's good they thought I was robbed; it could help me explain things if needed.

"How long have I been here?"

"This is your sixth day. You have been in a coma since you arrived, and the police have stopped by every day hoping to see you. Should I send them in now?"

"No! I mean not now, please. I'm not ready. Please."

"Okay. I'll tell them you've still not come around."

She started to walk away.

"Could you please tell me your name?" I asked.

"Nurse Blackwell, sir."

"Thank you, Nurse Blackwell. I'm in your debt."

She laughed and responded, "You certainly are, sir."

How long could I stall the police? I had no ID, no address, and no visible means of support. I could be jailed for vagrancy. The longer I interfaced with police, the worse it could get. If I told the truth, I'd spend the rest of my days in some funny farm in the past. I knew but one thing: I had to escape from there. I tried to stand, but my legs gave out, and I struggled just to get back into the bed. I guessed it wouldn't be today.

I faded in and out of sleep the rest of the day. The next morning, Nurse Blackwell returned to check my vitals, give me some medication, and inform me that breakfast was on its way. Oh yes, and sometime after breakfast, she would return to give me a sponge bath.

"Nurse, are the police still out there?"

"No, they have not been here yet today."

"Please don't let them see me. I need time to … I just need more time."

"Yes, Mr. Nixon."

"What? Oh yes." She had momentarily caught me off guard when she hit me with my newfound alias.

She left with a puzzled look on her face, and I just tried to smile.

After she left, I tried to stand. I was a little wobbly at first, but with a little perseverance, I soon got my legs back under me and was ready to grab my clothes and make my escape. However, I heard talking and the rattling of metal, so I quickly jumped back in bed, as that had to be breakfast coming. I was hungry, and I wasn't sure if there was any money in my trousers or not. But I never had a wallet, which was why the police thought it was stolen. So I ate everything. And when the nurse returned to collect the tray, I asked for more.

"Okay, mister." She was laughing. "But that's a first for me. Ain't no one ever asked for seconds on this stuff."

She continued to laugh as she went out the door, and when she came back with the food and left again, she was still chuckling. I ate quickly and then jumped up to see if the coast was clear. When it was, I jumped into my clothes, but when I pulled open the door to make a break for it, there stood a surprised cop. Oh, I knew he was a cop in spite of his plain clothes. His wrinkled gray suit, slightly wrinkled white shirt, scuffed shoes, and the fedora pushed back on his head gave it away. He was tall and fat with dark features and had a limp. In addition, he had bad breath and a bad attitude, and he chewed on half an unlit cigar.

"Going somewhere, Mr. Nixon? That is your name, isn't it? *Hmm?*"

"Well, to tell you the truth, yes."

"Yes, you're going somewhere, or yes, you're Mr. Nixon? *Hmm?*"

"Ah …"

"Mr. Nixon, why don't we step back inside your room, and we'll have a little chat, *hmm?*"

"Yes, why not," I responded without much enthusiasm as I walked back inside. My mind raced to come up with a story to keep me out of the clink or off the funny farm.

"Now, Mr. Nixon, aren't you interested in getting your wallet back, *hmm?*"

"Actually not if it means I must stay around here any longer. They only got a few dollars, and I need to get back to Dallas as soon as possible."

"So tell me, what are you doing here in DC, *hmm?*"

"I was meeting a friend who was giving me a ride back when those creeps shot me. He must have come for me after I was taken here and figured I found another ride and went on without me."

"Does this friend of yours have a name, *hmm?*"

This cop was most irritating with his little *hmm* at the end of each query.

"Yeah, his name is Dwight David Eisenhower." I could hardly keep a straight face.

"Do you have an address or phone number for this Mr. Dwight David Eisenhower, *hmm?*"

"No, I'm afraid I don't."

I really wanted to pop this guy and leave, but good luck smiled upon me when the attractive Nurse Blackwell came back in and told him to wait outside because it was time for my bath.

He looked very unhappy about that as he rolled the chewed-up cigar to the other side of his mouth and back again. "I'll be back, and you stay put," he grumbled as he pointed his fat finger at me and then limped out of the room.

"I'm sorry I wasn't here to stop him, but you're safe now."

"May I ask your first name, Nurse Blackwell?"

"It's Bonnie."

"Well, thank you, Bonnie. You are very kind, and you've saved me once again."

She smiled and said, "Okay, off with the clothes and back into your gown so I can bathe you."

"Yes, ma'am."

"Where did you think you were going? The doctor hasn't released you yet."

"Look, Bonnie, I can't explain, but trust me—I've got to get out of here. My life is in great danger if I don't get out of here very soon." I knew that was a bit of a stretch, but I had a feeling that if she wasn't on my side, I'd never make it.

I walked to the closet, changed, and got back into bed. She then washed me, all of me. It felt good. The water was warm, and her touch was gentle. It made me think of Julie. When I got an erection, I was so embarrassed. "I'm sorry."

She chuckled a bit. "You don't need to be. It happens to most of the men when they're bathed like this. Be glad; it means you're getting back to normal." She finished up and started to leave.

"Good-bye, Bonnie. It's been nice knowing you."

She gave me a look, the kind of look that seemed to suggest that she was not about to let me leave without doctor's orders. But I was leaving and just needed to say good-bye. I was now familiar with the timing for baths, food, medicine, etc. I knew it was time, and I was ready to make my break. I thought I'd never see her again. I was about to be proven wrong.

I had to get out of there and away from that cop. He was trouble for me with a capital T! After she finished, I waited a few minutes and then checked the hallway again. Now there was a uniformed officer sitting outside my door. So I dressed again and pulled my gown back over my clothes. I rolled my pants up so they didn't hang below the hem of the gown and wrapped a towel around my neck so my collar wouldn't show. I left my hat behind and stuffed my socks inside my shoes. Then I tucked the toe portion of the shoes under my waistband, with the heels resting on the top of the waistband. Then I tightened my belt under the heels to hold everything in place under the gown.

I waited for him to go to the water fountain, or somewhere just long enough for me to get out of there. Finally, he walked to the nurses' station to the right, and I headed for the men's room to the left and ducked inside. I shed the gown in a toilet stall, put on my shoes and socks, rolled down my pant legs, and when I came out, the officer was back in his chair reading a magazine, none the wiser that I had flown the coop. I strolled casually right out the side door. As I stood there trying to get my bearings, the door opened behind me. I was relieved when I saw it was Bonnie.

"Get in that black Ford Coupe across the parking lot, under the big elm tree, and stay down so no one will see you. I get off in an hour."

I nodded and walked to the parking lot in a roundabout way. I spotted the car and quickly slipped inside of it and locked the door. I detected a slight hint of her perfume inside the car, a sweet but delicate scent that I had noticed on her when she got near me. To be absolutely sure, I checked the registration on the back of the sun visor. Yep, that was Bonnie Blackwell's car all right. Now I was sure I had the right car. It seemed Ford had sold a lot of those black coupes that year, and I couldn't afford to be in the wrong one.

The car also had that new-car smell, and the registration said it was a 1937. Inside the car was empty but for a coffee mug, a red scarf with some white designs on it, and a well-worn, hardbound copy of a 1898 novel by HG Wells titled *War of the Worlds*. I chuckled when I read the title. That book wouldn't get much notoriety until October 30, 1938, when a young actor named Orson Welles and the Mercury Theater on the air would broadcast it as a news report, scaring thousands of people into believing we were being invaded by Martians. It was quite amusing to think of that.

A man dressed like a doctor came walking toward the car, so I slumped down so I wouldn't be seen. I really didn't want to be found. After he passed, I slid over the seat into the back and lay there until Bonnie got off work. It seemed like a very long hour, but eventually she came out and started to drive. When I saw her coming toward the car, I noticed she was carrying a large, paper grocery bag, and when she got into the car, she handed it to me. Inside was my hat. In this era, it wasn't common to see an adult male outside without a hat. It also had my journal. I had forgotten about that, and then it hit me—I always carried it inside my pants and under my shirt for fear of losing it. I looked at her. "How did you get this journal, and have you read it?"

"It was with your clothes in your room. When the police started asking questions and you seemed very uncomfortable with them about, I retrieved it and kept it in my locker. I'm not really sure why I did it—just a feeling I guess. I kept meaning to ask you about it, but it seemed when I thought about it, you were either asleep or that cop was around. As far as reading it, oh boy, was I tempted, but I didn't. Should I have?"

"No, not yet anyway—I mean, maybe someday. It's not that interesting." Smart lady, but now I had her involved.

"Why did you do this for me?"

She laughed and said, "Seems I'm the gal who's always picking up stray dogs and cats. Just a sucker for anything or anyone down on their luck.

I trust you are not some kind of criminal and I haven't just put myself in harm's way, *hmm?*"

"No, I am definitely not any kind of criminal."

"Well then, no need to worry, right?"

I nodded, and as she continued to drive, we both laughed at her imitation of the way the flatfoot spoke, the one who had been busting my chops.

"You can drop me at the nearest inexpensive motel, if it's not out of your way."

"Nonsense. You're coming home with me and have a good meal and good night's sleep. I have a spare room you may use until we figure out how to get you back to Dallas."

"Oh, that's very kind of you, but you don't need to bother yourself with me. Besides, I have no money to pay you."

She turned into a market, parked, and turned off the car.

"That is exactly my point. You have no money, and around here you will be picked up for vagrancy and jailed. Do you want your friend from the hospital to find you, *hmm?*"

Once again we both laughed at her attempt to imitate that fat cop's manner of speech.

"But really, I could be some mad serial killer for all you know."

"We already covered that point, and you promised you were not a bad man, right?"

"Yes, but would such a person admit to it?"

"Look, Mr. Richard Nixon, you need help, and I am able to give it. I wouldn't be much of a Christian if I didn't help when I could. No, sir, you're coming with me, and that's final. Now I must go in this store and pick up something for dinner. Can I trust you to wait here quietly and stay out of sight? I'll only be a minute."

"Yes, ma'am. I shall follow your instructions to the letter."

I did as she asked. It was now a little past 1400, and I hoped she didn't live far away from the Mayflower. I wondered if Sheila would remember to tell Doc to look for the trunk and if he would build the pod and bring me back. I would have no way of knowing when it was 1980 there. I thought it was now. I was in real time here, but I was in 1980 when I left, so maybe he'd had his forty-three years with Sheila, and now he was discovering the trunk. I had to get to the beam-in point by midnight and noon as often as possible just in case. I mean, the United States was safe, and he should be able to get new fuel, right? That was my only hope.

Bonnie returned with a bag of groceries and smiled as she started the car.

"Do you live far from the Mayflower, Bonnie?"

"No. Actually, I live just about three miles from there."

"Do you live alone?"

"Yes. Nobody but me and the occasional stray," she said with a wink and a smile.

Several minutes later, she pulled into the driveway of the cutest bungalow-style house I had ever seen. A white picket fence surrounded the entire house. The large, covered front porch had two swings, one on each side of the front steps. Both faced out toward the street and were built for two or three people. The flowerbeds on either side of the front steps were filled with tulips, daffodils, and crocus. They were all beautiful, and there were rose bushes that were beginning to show early signs of budding. A single tree adorned the front yard, a medium-sized magnolia, and I could almost smell the sweet fragrance of summer.

As we walked through the front door to the foyer, hardwood floors sparkled beneath my feet, and the light tan walls accented by white dental and crown molding gave the room a feel of elegance. The dining room had a matching chair rail. The old-fashioned appliances of the kitchen were bright white, and they looked only a couple of years old. She kept the home immaculate.

"Bonnie, do you have a housekeeper?"

"Why no, I can't afford that. Why do you ask?"

"You home is so beautiful and well kept. How do you manage to keep it so and work full-time?"

"I usually do a little each day, and then on my days off, I really give it a good going over. Thank you for noticing. Would you like to freshen up?"

"Yes, but it seems I have nothing but the clothes on my back."

She turned, looked me up and down, and then said, "There are some men's clothes in the closet of the room you will be using. Let me show you."

Bonnie led me upstairs into a really nice room with a large double bed, a dresser, and two nightstands. She opened the closet door and revealed a closet full of men's clothes.

"Did these belong to a husband or boyfriend? Perhaps the man who owns them might not care for me wearing them."

She looked at me strangely, and I recognized that look immediately. My thinking was in 1980, but she was here in 1937. Living with a man she wasn't wedded to in 1980 was no big deal, but in 1937, the social mores in the country in those days would not look kindly upon a woman who lived such a lifestyle. She quickly straightened out my thinking.

"No, they belonged to my father, and he was about your size. He died six months ago. I can't bring myself to part with them, and my mother wouldn't have them around to remind her of his being gone."

"I'm sorry. I didn't mean—"

She cut me off. "No problem, Richard. For some reason not yet known to me, I believe you meant no disrespect. Freshen up, help yourself to any of the clothes, and come down in thirty minutes, and supper will be ready."

Red-faced, I thanked her and said I'd be right down.

When I returned to the dining room, she said, "Well, Richard, you look refreshed." It seemed strange hearing her call me Richard. I had to at least set that straight. After she sat down and all the food was on the table, she asked if I would mind if she said grace. I smiled, folded my hands, and bowed my head.

When she finished, I said, "Bonnie, there's something I must tell you right away."

She laid her napkin across her lap and looked up. "Let me guess, your name isn't Richard Nixon?"

I looked up with utter shock. *She did read my journal* was my first thought.

"No, I'm not a mind reader, but it was the way you looked at me when I called you Richard. Oh, I can't describe the look, but it just wasn't natural. Most people like it when you say their name, but your reaction was different somehow. Besides, you don't look like a Richard."

"Wow, that's amazing. Why didn't you say something before?"

"I figured you would tell me when you were ready. So, what is your name, sir?"

She had made it easier by telling me that she knew and she wasn't upset with me. "It's Jake, Jake Kincannon, and I'm a private investigator—or at least I was."

"Well, Mr. Jake Kincannon, it's nice to meet you, and let's eat before it's cold."

"Yes, good idea."

Bonnie had cooked a great dinner that night, and it felt good to have a friend in this strange world that was not my own. We talked for hours before we retired to our bedrooms for the night.

She didn't have much in the way of pictures, though. She told me she had no family, save her mom; she had never been married, thus no kids. In addition, her father had died in an automobile accident, and her mom now lived in Frederick, Maryland, which she said was about a two-and-a-half-hour drive. She said she would go spend a weekend with her when she could, usually about every other month, plus Thanksgiving and Christmas. She liked to garden and work around the house, and she had a local girlfriend she would go out with occasionally. She wanted to eventually meet a good man, settle down, and have kids. However, there were no real prospects in sight. She told me the last guy she dated was a doctor from the hospital where she worked, but that didn't last long because he had wanted more than she was willing to give. I suspected that I knew what she meant.

She took good care of me, and she took me to the beam point whenever she could, and she never questioned why I had to go there after the first time when I told her it wasn't safe for her to know the answer to that query. But I promised her, again, that I was not a fugitive or a gangster of any type. If she was working a shift and couldn't take me, I just couldn't get there. Fortunately for me, she had enough seniority that she usually worked the dayshift.

Doc said I might never get back, but I was banking on Sheila giving Doc the message and Doc being just curious enough to go into the attic to see what she was talking about. So I had to keep trying, keep going to the beam point and standing there at midnight or noon, whenever I could arrange to get there. Being optimistic, I had written a farewell letter to Bonnie, and whenever she rode me to the beam point, it was in my dresser drawer on top of my socks ... I mean, her dad's socks. When I returned, disappointed that I was still in 1937, I hid it.

I had lost my suitcase, left it in my room at the Mayflower when I had to make a hasty exit from there the night I saved Sheila. I didn't explain to Bonnie why I had no earthly possessions, and she never asked. That was very perceptive of her not to ask, but surely she must have been curious. Someday I would have to tell her if I continued to live under her roof. She also never questioned my strange ritual of going to an alley behind the Mayflower and a few minutes later returning and riding home again.

I wondered, if I ever got back to my time and looked her up, would she know me? Would she have some distant memory of a strange patient that became her ward, had no possessions, seemed to come without a past, and then one day disappeared as mysteriously as he had appeared? Silly thought, I guess, but hell, what else did I have to think about in limbo land?

Each trip to the beam point ended in the same way. I would come back to her house feeling depressed and angry. Angry at being stuck there for sure, but oddly, mostly angry with Sheila, as she was the one who supposedly knew of me. Yet she hadn't done anything to push Doc to bring me home. But then, when would she tell Doc and when would he start building the Teleporter, if at all? Really, I couldn't be sure of anything that was happening there. At least my hostess, Bonnie, was everything a person in my position could ask for and more.

Days turned into weeks, and whenever I stood on the beam point, be it at noon or midnight, nothing happened. Each time I told myself the next time would be the time, but I still got angry each time I was still there after the appointed time had passed. But I went faithfully back at the next opportunity. However, after about the twentieth or so time of going to the beam point, failing to end up back in my own time, and becoming angrier with each failed attempt, I decided it was time to accept the fact that I was likely there for the duration of my life. I would still go to the beam point, but I would not dwell on it. If one day I disappeared, well, so be it.

All I could do was hope that something changed to get Doc to find the trunk and build the machine and get me home. Meanwhile, I would try to find a job and be productive. I felt like a lowlife sponging off a nice person like Bonnie. I knew Doc had all the info to quickly build the Teleporter, if Sheila remembered to give him a reason.

CHAPTER 19

ON THE OTHER SIDE OF TIME

As I drove back to Bonnie's house from another disappointment at the beam point, I thought about what was happening with Doc and Sheila. They were there alongside me in 1937. I knew Sheila, and she knew me, and she knew I was from the future and had to get back there. They had already moved to Chicago. Sheila would remember what happened only a few weeks ago. I could pick up the phone and call her, but I wouldn't; it could change history in some way I couldn't fix, and then I might never get home to my time. I had to trust she would do as she promised. They had to live out forty-three years to get to my time. I would grow old with them unless and until they pulled me back through time in the Teleporter. When Sheila went home on the night in 1937, she didn't go home in the original history. Time for Doc would have changed. He wouldn't be sitting or sleeping at his desk, waiting for the moment when history would change. Just prior to saving Sheila, he would have thought he would never see me again, but hopefully Sheila would be my savior.

At the moment in history when Sheila didn't die, everything would have changed. Doc would no longer be in that basement, but instead in their bed at the home of Professor and Mrs. Wilson J. Wells in Mount Vernon, Virginia. That was, if I understood this time travel stuff. She likely pulled into her driveway, parked the car, quietly entered the house, did whatever she did before retiring for the night, and slipped between the covers with Doc. Something I would give anything to be doing with Julie right then. When Doc awoke on that history-changed day, it would be his brand-new life. In my time of 1980, it would be them as an old married couple with forty-three additional years of fond memories.

Sheila would know that I saved her, but would she really believe that I was from the future, sent by her husband in 1980 for that purpose? Only time would tell. I could see Sheila driving home from the Pentagon that fateful night and them relocating to Chicago, a changed life for both, but to each in a different way. They would move into Doc's father's house that he inherited along with the office building where Doc and I had first met. Now a life they had never known was about to play out before them. Hopefully it would be a wonderful life filled with great memories, as Doc had spent so many years to rescue her. The years would hopefully ease her knowledge of the close call with death and her time spent as a spy for the United States government, but not of me. The change Doc and I had brought about was a good thing, except for the obvious—my life as I knew it was there, and I was stuck here.

Maybe Doc would wake up as he heard the sounds of someone entering the house. He would likely fumble for the lamp on the nightstand. When he finally found it, he would see Sheila coming home as usual and perhaps might wait patiently in a king-sized bed in a beautifully decorated bedroom to sample his wife's kisses. His mind would be filled with only one memory. He would know a second set once Sheila told him of it and forced him to retrieve one of the hidden trunks.

Sheila was safe, at least from the original horror of her past, but it still remained a slight possibility that whatever it was that we did that allowed the Nazis to win the war was still messed up, and I would live through a different ending than should have been. They would return to bed and fall asleep with Doc insisting on holding her hand after Sheila pushed off his sexual advances and told him it was too late for fooling around. I was sure that Sheila's memory of what originally happened would fade into oblivion through the years. Until then, I had to begin to function like a normal person living in 1937. At least I had the comfort of knowing that in WWII, we would ultimately win and rid the world of Hitler, Mussolini, and the emperor of Japan.

Doc and Sheila would wake the next morning to a new day, a day that wasn't out of the ordinary for them. However, Sheila would have to carry the lie of what she had done for that relatively short period of time when she was a double agent. Her telling him what she had done for God and country and with Hans, when I saved her without killing Hans, had been wiped from Doc's memory, as it didn't happen. I wondered if she would have to tell him everything this time to get him to build it.

In 1980, they had damn well better bring me home and return my life as I knew it and at the age I was when I left, which he could do thanks to that time warping ability Doc spoke of so proudly.

Then I remembered Julie. Would she somehow be a part of this equation? Would I be no one to her? Probably, but I would have all these memories—memories of Julie and all we shared for our time together; of learning that Sheila wasn't kidnapped, as Doc thought for many years, none of which he now knew of; of the Nazis ruling the world; and of Bonnie and whatever would happen to me until I got back to my old life, if I ever did. Each time I went to the beam point and nothing happened, I became more discouraged.

I stopped all the daydreaming as I pulled into Bonnie's driveway.

Time moved on, and weeks had now turned to months. Spring had turned to summer and now to fall. I faithfully made my treks as often as possible in hopes of one day getting home. The one and only thing I'd had on me when I left the Mayflower that night was my journal, since I always kept it inside my shirt, under my belt. I was glad I still had it. It would help me remember the things that had happened to me in both time frames, in 1937 and in 1980. It might also make interesting reading for Julie upon my eventual return home.

One day, I was writing in my journal, and my alarm signaled that the time to drive to the beam point had come. I looked outside, saw it was snowing, and said, "To hell with it. What's the use?"

I didn't go. Then I felt tremendous guilt and regret after hearing Bonnie's clock chime noon. Hope of returning was beginning to fade, and Bonnie was becoming more important to me with each month that passed. I wrote off my feelings for her as just a port in the storm, but each time I stood on the beam point at the appointed times and held my breath, awaiting that familiar stomach-lifting experience to occur, and then nothing happened, my hopes of returning slipped away a little more.

A few weeks later as she got ready for work, I made some coffee and had a light breakfast ready for her by the time she came downstairs. As we sat there,

I noticed how much I enjoyed doing things for her. I sipped my coffee and watched her eat. I thought how beautiful she was, not only on the outside, but I had learned over the months that she was equally beautiful on the inside. "Bonnie, I can't keep living off you. I need to find work to pay my way."

After telling her my real name shortly after I moved in with her, I also told her where I was from. It was a believable *where* I was from, just not *when* I was from. Sure, I wanted to tell her, but how could I? How could she ever believe such a fantastic story?

"Jake, wait. You've taken care of the house, the yard, the cooking, and my car. You have become a friend and companion, and frankly I have never felt safer than with you around. Not to mention, you're my favorite movie companion and someone to go out to dinner with. It's no fun alone. To me, you have more than earned your keep, what little keep there is. You sleep in a room that was empty before. No expense there. The food you eat is what was usually wasted before, so little expense there. So I think I have the best of the arrangement."

"That's kind of you to say, but I'm also interfering with your life. With me hanging around, how can you find a man to learn to love and to give you a family?"

"That's a long way from being a priority with me, but when the time comes, I'll boot you out," she said with a smile as she stood up and then kissed my forehead. "See you tonight, roomie."

"Yeah, see ya." A funny feeling shot through me when she said "*boot you out.*"

I cleaned the house and washed all the dishes. It was how I appeased my conscience for being a freeloader. I rewrote my farewell letter ... again. Interestingly, it became harder and harder to write it. But it seemed necessary as we learned more and more of each other and events happened. I left it on the top of my dresser, as I did every time, thinking—perhaps hoping—not to return. When 1100 came, I hitchhiked to the beam point. Some days I'd catch a ride, some days only a partial. The Mayflower was a good hike even in the best conditions. There I'd stand on my spot and watch as high noon came and went. Then I had the joy of hitchhiking or walking back to Bonnie's. Sometimes I wouldn't be home much before she was. On many days, I would drive Bonnie to work and use her car to get there and then pick her up at the end of her shift.

My other life was fading in my mind, and I was now beginning to resign myself to the fact that I was here for the duration of my life. Not much of a life when you knew everything that was going to happen before it happened. The few events I'd shared with Bonnie had her thinking I was a very smart man. But I was a fraud trying to keep the hope alive that I was going home, and I had to make the best of what I could here. I figured I should really forget all that was before and see if I could make Bonnie happy and spend my life with her. After all, she rescued me. I definitely sensed an attraction, but more from her than from me.

I began to laugh out loud and then said out loud, perhaps expecting someone to hear me, "I was sent to rescue Sheila, and I did, only to be forgotten by the people who said they would never forget. I'm angry with all of you, but mostly Sheila. Now I'm here, stuck in a time not of my own choosing, and have been rescued by a wonderful woman who asks nothing or seems to expect nothing from me, just to take care of me. How ironic!"

Bonnie was and had been so good to me, and I was ashamed that I had been living off her. So far we had remained good friends and nothing more. However, I suspected she had started to have feelings for me, and I couldn't return them. Yeah, I was very lonely, and it would have been so easy to fall into her arms and make love to her. In fact, some nights I could barely keep myself from going to her bed. On those nights, I would try hard to focus on Julie and not think about what was only a few steps away.

But I wondered how long I could withstand those manly urges with a healthy, well-built woman across the hall. It was only the hope of getting home that stopped me. I knew if I made that trip across the hall, I would have to resign myself to stay forever. It may have been the eighties in my head, but she was a gal of the thirties, and I just couldn't hurt her in any way. But the thoughts of her in my mind got stronger and stronger while the prospects of getting home grew fainter and fainter. I was barely able to picture Julie in my mind; she was literally fading away.

Then a few weeks later, it happened. It was the week before Thanksgiving. I started the day as usual when she worked the dayshift, which she was doing more and more as her seniority grew. I cooked her breakfast and made us coffee, as usual.

When she came and sat down, I said, "I have to tell you something. I have to find work."

"Jake, we've been through this. You do more than enough already. Plus, you can't risk getting caught without ID. I couldn't bear to see you in jail."

"But, Bonnie, I can't live like this, and besides, I'm trying to get home, and I can't—"

She cut me off with a surprised look. "What do you mean trying to get home?"

"It's a long story, and you don't have time to listen now, but when you come home tonight, I'll tell you everything. I promise—everything."

She wanted to pursue the conversation, but I insisted she go to work or else she might lose her job, and we would both starve to death. I kissed her forehead and sent her on her way. It seemed we were always kissing each other on the forehead. She went but wearing the most perplexed look I had ever seen on a person.

Once again I did my chore duties, and at the same time as every day, I headed for the hotel to do what was fast becoming my ridiculous ritual. Once again, I stepped on the spot that should have taken me home long ago, and once again nothing happened, so I asked for the directions to the department for obtaining an automobile license.

They gave me a very short written test and had me drive a police officer around. Then they typed up my license. That was the official end to Mr. Richard Nixon and the beginning of the legitimacy of one stranger to town, Mr. John Jake Kincannon, a.k.a. Jake Kincannon. Now I was somebody, and I had a license to prove it. I chuckled to myself when I looked at the made-up birth date on my new license. Why, I wasn't even born yet. That thought made me wonder about my parents. I was born in 1947, and at that time my dad was twenty-six, and my mom was twenty-three, so today they would be sixteen and thirteen, respectively. Wow! If I were to fly to Chicago in this time period and look them up, they would be in high school. Wouldn't that be a stitch to talk to them? I was older than my parents!

I continued to toss those thoughts around in my head as I walked down to the local newspaper office and asked to see their news morgue. They sat me down, and I began combing through the recent help-wanted ads. I found a couple jobs that sounded like the companies were small enough that they wouldn't be too picky about my credentials. One didn't pan out, but I was able to secure a job working on an assembly line for a small manufacturing company. My gross pay was twenty dollars a week. In my time, 1980, that was closer to an hourly wage than weekly. Unbelievable, but then costs of goods here were in line with wages. They hadn't heard the word inflation yet, but the young ones would.

They gave me the title of machinist. I found that somewhat curious. I had just showed them my new driver's license and filled out an information form, and they seemed satisfied. I was to start in two days. I hoped Bonnie would be pleased. The hours would have me home when she got home on days she worked the dayshift.

I returned home at about 1600 and heard the phone ringing. It turned out to be Bonnie. She told me some tragic news about a bad fire; they were bringing in a lot of burn victims, and she might have to stay as late as midnight. I asked if she would pick me up at the hotel, since I would be there for my usual rendezvous at midnight.

That night, I arrived at 2330, putting me there ahead of her by mere minutes. When she pulled up, we talked about the fire and her day until the bewitching moment was at hand. I stepped onto the beam point a few seconds before midnight. As Bonnie watched me do my ceremonial ritual, and as I watched the second hand of my watch approach twelve, all of a sudden, I hoped I wouldn't leave. And of course, I didn't. I jumped back into her car feeling strangely euphoric.

Bonnie, as usual, said nothing, expecting me to be sad and quiet, per usual. Instead, I suggested we stop off for a drink at Mike's, a quiet, little bar I had found and frequented some nights when I hitchhiked home from the beam point. I usually stopped to drink away my sorrows, but never got drunk; somehow I knew Bonnie would not approve. Tonight was different. I wanted to be with her, just her. No sadness, just contentment, celebration even. I told her the celebration was because I now had a driver's license and had found a job that day.

"What's come over you, Jake? You're usually quiet when you leave the place you stand, that place I'm not supposed to ask about. If it's the job, I guess I should have pushed you to do it long ago."

"Things are changing, but we won't discuss that tonight. It's the holiday season, and I want to have some good cheer with a most important person in my life."

She smiled like I hadn't seen her smile before as she nodded and said, "That's the best thing I've heard in a long time. I'll drink to that."

She wheeled the car into Mike's parking lot, and in we went. We grabbed a small booth in the corner beside a Christmas tree that was already in place. The glow of the soft tree lights made this wonderful woman breathtaking to behold. I had never really looked at her in the way I was that night, in that bar, beside that glorious tree. We had never talked so much before, on this slightly more intimate level, and I learned all about her. I was sure she had told me these things before, but I guessed I hadn't really been listening with the same ears I listened with tonight. This was without a doubt the best night I'd had since … well, since before.

Tonight I would take this luscious woman into my arms and seal my fate with a kiss, and our bodies would start a new life for us. So we had a couple drinks each and then headed home. When we walked inside, it felt warm and cozy like I had never noticed before. After we removed our coats and hung them up, I could wait no longer. I took her arm, spun her around gently, and pulled her into my arms. She felt so good in my arms, but she put her hands on my shoulders as I tried to pull her in for that fateful kiss.

"No, Jake. No, stop. Listen to me for a second. I know I have not been able to hide my feelings from you successfully, and I want this more than you know, but it can't happen. It can't happen until I know what mystery lies between us with these twice-daily trips of yours. My heart and head disagree on this point, but for now, my head is winning."

It was as if she had thrown ice water on a red-hot poker; I could almost hear the sizzling sound. It sobered me up, and I felt bad. After all, I've been very involved with a young lady I thought I loved, but she's in another time, a time I'll likely never see again.

I backed off and said, "I promised to tell you everything, and I will, but you've had a really long day. Could it wait till morning?"

"As much as I want to hear it now, I suspect you are right. The long day has mixed with the alcohol and emotion, and I might fall asleep in the middle of this story of yours."

"I thank you for not insisting, Bonnie."

We went to kiss each other on the forehead, but our lips touched lightly instead. We both knew the danger there, and she pulled away very quickly, before events got out of control and consumed us in a fiery passion. That didn't help me sleep. I thought about how that quick encounter with her lips felt and then about what her reaction would be to the tale I would have to tell her come morning. I wasn't sure at that particular moment if I loved Bonnie or was mad at Julie for abandoning me. Wow, what a brain session I had with myself. Then I heard the door open, and my bedroom light came on. It was Bonnie. I looked at my alarm clock to see it was only 0500.

"I just woke up and can't get back to sleep until I know what *'going home'* is all about," she said with her hands on her hips and a worried look on her face.

I sat up quickly and suggested we get some coffee and talk about it. She nodded, and we each took a turn in the bathroom and then headed for the kitchen.

"I think you'd better sit down because you may find the truth stranger than fiction."

I poured us each a cup of coffee and sat down. "Okay, at the risk of being ordered to leave, here goes." I paused for her to take a sip of coffee and set her cup down. "I am from the future."

With that, her jaw dropped open. Then she smirked in disbelief, but she let me continue. "I'm sorry for saying what I said without explanation, but I will now tell you everything. I ask only that you let me tell it my way and take me to that hotel once more before I conclude it. Okay?"

I told her about my business, I told her about Doc and his machine, I told her about Doc's wife and her role in the coming war with Germany. It was now November 1937, and I told her that air and naval forces from the Empire of Japan would attack the naval station at Pearl Harbor on December 7, 1941, and that on December 11, 1941, we would officially declare war on Germany. I hated to tell her those things, but I had to convince her that I was, in fact, from the future. Granted, she would not see this for three years. So I told her things I remembered from the history of that era to prove myself. I told her all I could at that point, but not about Julie. I spoke of her only as my gal Friday. I couldn't tell her about that, at least not until I had her believing me.

By the time we drank several cups of coffee and discussed all that I had to tell her and I had answered all her questions to the best of my ability, it was time to gauge her reaction. The only way was to hold her in my arms. If she rejected me, we were doomed, and I would most likely be asked to leave. On the other hand, if she believed me, maybe we could have a life together.

I stood before her, gently held her arms, and lifted her to her feet. I stared deeply into her eyes and read them as a green light. I slowly pulled her close, and we kissed fully, firmly, and with so much pent-up passion that we damn near didn't make it back up the stairs to her bedroom. By the time we hit the bed, we were almost nude, save underwear. Her body was mature, firm, and as soft as one could imagine. Her breasts were the perfect size, with large, pink nipples that stood hard from excitement. Her well-developed legs surrounded me as if to say, "You ain't going nowhere but here." She moaned softly as I penetrated her with bold but tender moves. It wasn't long before the explosion of sexual wonderment took us both to heaven and back. When we finally collapsed in each other's arms, she was all dewy and sweet. It was obvious to each of us that this was definitely where we would stay.

Tears started to slide down her cheeks as she confessed to me that she had loved me the day she first saw me. I couldn't say the same, but then, I didn't have the singleness of mind and purpose she had.

I could not refuse, so I kissed her long and softly. *Necking* was the universal term of my day. We pulled apart only because we both heard the clock in her hallway strike noon.

I laughed and said, "Well, you won't have to take me to that hotel ever again."

We both laughed and then spent the rest of that day in and out of each other's minds and arms. Bonnie's long day the day before had earned her this day off. She called her supervisor and asked to trade for the nightshift starting the next night. It seemed she felt that we should not be under the roof of her house at night. Neither of us would be able to sleep alone again, and given the fact that we were unmarried ... Well, let's just say the times, they would be a changin', as Bob Dylan would sing someday in the future. I didn't want us to pass like ships in the night, so I asked her at breakfast if she would do me the honor of becoming Mrs. Kincannon. She agreed. Perhaps it was selfish. Perhaps it was a confirmation that this was now my life and I would never step back into my old one. I loved her, and I was ready to be with the woman of this time and step up to be a man worthy of this fine, loving woman. As Shakespeare said in the *Tempest*, "What was past is prologue."

I went out and bought her an inexpensive, gold engagement ring with one small diamond and its matching gold wedding band. We kept separate bedrooms, which reminded me of Julie; seems both the women I loved were maintaining this same kind of barrier. Maybe that was to keep me from having everything until I made honest women out of them.

Soon, Thanksgiving was upon us, and we visited and I finally met her mom. We had a great weekend, and we went back again to celebrate the birth of Christ holiday with her. New Year's Eve was another story; that we kept all for ourselves.

We kissed and hugged at midnight and toasted with glasses of champagne. I turned to the fireplace with my back to Bonnie and stared at the fire. My thoughts were quickly consumed with thoughts of my other life. I wondered what Julie was doing at this very minute. What about Doc and Sheila? Did she tell him about me? Were they talking about me?

Bonnie put her hand on my shoulder and said, "Are you in the future?" She was so perceptive, almost like she could read my mind.

I turned with a smile and said, "No, darling, I'm just toasting the end of a life and the beginning of a new one." I touched my glass to hers lightly and said, "Here's looking at you, kid." Then I took the last sip and smashed the glass into the fireplace. She followed suit. We kissed passionately and then held each other and watched 1937 give way to 1938 as the radio played "Auld Lang Syne," and the fire crackled and flickered brightly. It was symbolic and the final untethering of me from the past—or should I say future.

It almost seemed like overnight. I brought out the gold band and later hired a minister in a small Lutheran church to perform the ceremony after the morning Christmas service, and on December 25, 1938, we were married. Could one find a more joyous day of the year to be married? Interestingly, there I was, an adult marrying this wonderful woman, and as the year 1938 wound to an end, my mother and father hadn't even met yet. Nineteen eighty was like a dream that vanished with a new day. Julie, my sweet Julie, was now just a far distant and very faded memory. When I tried to picture Julie in one of our intimate moments, all I could see was Bonnie. It was as though what Julie and I had done was really Bonnie and I. The mind was a fascinating place.

CHAPTER 20

THE SHORES OF HOME

What had been my temporary refuge in what seemed like a foreign land had now become my home. I would never see the shores of home again. This time was now my time, Bonnie's home was now our home, and Bonnie was now my love. I knew I would never again return to that spot of asphalt in the alley behind the Mayflower Hotel, where I had been so many times before.

My life as Jake Kincannon, PI, was over. Now I was Jake Kincannon. I didn't know what would become of me—professionally, that is. I was now, temporarily, a machinist and the former roommate of one Bonnie Blackwell, RN, now Bonnie Kincannon, RN. Now that we were married, the lovemaking flowed like water, and it seemed like our chief entertainment. I told her once that an old man I worked with in my other life had told me that I would make love to my wife more in the first year of our marriage than in all the other years combined. I laughed at that then and still found it unbelievable. We lived a modest life, but we were extremely happy.

One evening, we were lying in bed in each other's arms when out of the blue she said, "Jake, one thing bothers me. Last night I had this horrible dream that you went to see Doc and convinced him to build that machine, and one day you were gone. I know you told me you could never visit him, and he wouldn't remember you even if you did, but what if somehow, someway he builds it and pulls you back to 1980 and out of my life?"

"Darling, even if he builds that Teleporter tomorrow, it can't get me back if I don't step on the spot of asphalt you took me to so many times. I have no plans to be anywhere near that place anymore than I have plans to be with another woman."

"So what is it like to have lived in two different times? Is it like living a double life?"

"To me, it seems more like living in the past and dreaming about or reading a novel about the future. I suppose it could be the reverse as well."

"If you were the author of that novel, which way would you write it?"

"Oh, I don't know. Maybe both."

"Yeah well, when they make it into a movie, who will play me?"

"Ah, well let's see … Got it, the most beautiful actress in the world, and it would depend on when the movie was made. If it's in the forties, Rita Hayworth; the fifties, Kim Novak; the sixties; Natalie Wood."

"Who are these people?"

"They are, in my humble opinion, three absolutely gorgeous women, all actresses. I'm not sure which I like best, but it's between Kim and Natalie. I fell in love with Kim Novak when she danced with William Holden in the movie, *Picnic*. Then there's Natalie Wood. You know, *Splendor in the Grass, Gypsy,* and *This Property is Condemned* … Oh no, wait, you can't know. None of them are known in this time. Their time hasn't come yet, and that seems to happen to me a lot. I'm thinking about something or someone and then realize that it or they haven't happened yet."

I told their lives, at least as much as I knew. Rita the redhead, Kim the blonde, and Natalie the brunette. I always thought there was more to Natalie's death than a simple drowning. We talked of a few other oddities from the future until we drifted off to sleep.

The next morning, I awoke with a wild idea—write a book. I guess all that talk from the night before planted the seed that grew in my subconscious while I slept. It could be a futuristic fiction of what happened to me. I could name it *Going Home to the Future, Lost in the Past,* or *Coming Home from the Past* or some other wild title. The irony was that it would be an autobiography written as science fiction. The more I thought about it, the more I became enamored with the idea. I had made coffee and breakfast for Bonnie, which allowed her to eke out a few more minutes of sleep before getting ready for work and beginning her shift.

When she finally came downstairs and kissed me good morning, I sat her down with a cup of coffee, and as I put her breakfast on the plate, I told her of my idea.

"I think that's a great idea, honey!"

Her encouragement was all I needed. "All I need is a PC and I'm good … Oh wait, no PCs yet."

"What's a PC?"

"Personal computer."

She looked at me with a strange expression.

"Never mind. It's not available yet. Would you happen to have a typewriter here at the house?"

"Sure, there's one I used in college in the little bedroom closet shelf, all the way in the back. There should be some paper there also, but I'm not sure if the ribbon is any good … Oh gosh, look at the time. I've gotta run, babe."

The day was perfect for starting such an ambitious undertaking. It was heavily overcast, and it had been raining off and on the entire night. The radio said the rain would likely last all day. After Bonnie dashed off to work, I went looking for the typewriter. I found it and the paper right where she said it would be. I made another pot of coffee, tuned in some soothing music on the radio, and set up the typewriter at the dining room table, along with the stack of blank typing paper. Now the big question was if the old typewriter would still work.

Thankfully, I quickly discovered that the typewriter did work. So with everything in order and a mug of coffee at the ready, I sat down to start the great adventure of writing my novel. I never learned to type, so I employed the old hunt-and-peck system. I began pecking away, wondering if I could fill up enough pages. I used my journal to help keep the time line. The hours slipped away. It was a good thing I was off that day, or I would have missed half a day without realizing it. I only became cognizant of the time when I heard the afternoon newspaper hit the screen door and bang against the doorframe. That broke me out of the spell I was in. I couldn't believe I was so engrossed in the writing that most of the day had disappeared unnoticed.

I made a sandwich and drank a beer and then went back to the typewriter. The words were flowing, but with my lack of typing skill and the mistakes, it was slow sledding. Still, by the time Bonnie returned home from work, I had written thirty-five pages.

The next morning, our roles were reversed. She was off from work, and I had to go back. I was really tempted to call in sick so I could spend another day on my new avocation, but my wife assured me that was not a sound idea. We had a great way of handling our different work patterns. Whoever had the day off cooked breakfast. As she served me up eggs, grits, and toast and sat to keep me company, she told me she had read my manuscript. "It's very good, dear, but you said this was a true account of what happened to you?"

I nodded as I took another bite of my toast.

"You haven't embellished it in any way?"

"No, why?"

"Well, my dear, when you told me of your trip from the future, I believe you described Julie as your girl Friday. You omitted the other days of the week."

I damn near choked on breakfast. I began explaining, and I must have been tripping all over myself, as she soon began to laugh. I stopped talking and just looked at her.

"Darling, I'm kidding with you. I'm not insecure about us. It's just that you left that chapter out when you told me the story of the future and how you became stranded here. You of all people should know that if you didn't have a past, how could you have a future?"

I released my breath and felt the relief come over me, which she picked up on and which caused her to laugh even more, which in turn started me laughing. Admittedly, mine was more of a nervous laugh. We talked awhile longer until I had to rush so as not to be late on the job. I grabbed my lunch box, gave her a huge kiss, and headed off to work, and by the time I returned, Bonnie had retyped the pages and corrected some grammar and typos. Now there weren't all those little holes from wherever I tried to make an erasure. What a sweetheart she was. I also noted that she had put my author name down as Max Bonny. When I questioned her about it, she said she remembered I had told her somewhere along the line that I liked the name Max and as a kid had a dog named Max, and the Bonny was so I wouldn't forget her when I became rich and famous. We had a good laugh over that, but the name stuck as my pen name.

Soon I found myself writing while she fixed meals. I got up an hour or more before she did each day to work on this silly idea of mine. I slowly became hooked on this crazy book stuff. She said she looked forward to reading each day's work, and maybe that was part of it. I so much wanted to please her, and I was falling deeper in love with her with each day that passed. Bonnie said it was sort of like some of the radio dramas of the day where you had to "tune in tomorrow night for the exciting continuation of *General Hospital*" or a radio drama like *Sam Spade*. Bonnie was an avid reader of mystery and science-fiction books, so this was right up her alley, and she offered gentle critiques so as not to wound my male ego. Most of the time, I took those suggestions. There was an added bonus that she confessed one night as we lay in bed: she was learning more and more of my past.

Lying in bed while she read that day's writings became a sort of nightly event we both looked forward to—her for the reading, and me waiting anxiously for her comments and admiring her fabulous body as she lay there in her thin nightgown. She also continued to neatly retype what I had turned out previously when she had the time. It seemed like the more I wrote and she read, the more she continued to encourage me and cheer me on. Weeks turned into months, and we became happier and happier together, and the manuscript grew larger and larger.

One Friday night, as she was reading the story, she turned the page and came to those words so common to every novel: *The End*. She seemed genuinely sad that the story was over and suggested I write another.

I laughed and said, "You can't be serious."

"I'm very serious. You have a real flare for writing, and I think it's excellent."

"Babe, I did this as a lark, but your encouragement was what made me continue. But this was a whim, and then it became solely for your entertainment, as well as to let you know my life to this point."

"I think lots of folks would really enjoy this novel, and who knows, you may become rich and famous."

All I could do was laugh, but she didn't share my laughter. So I kissed her. One kiss led to another, and soon the discussion of my silly book faded into more pleasurable matters.

The next day was Saturday, and unfortunately, Bonnie had to work the dayshift, so we planned to go out that night, which was typically our date night anyway. After I fixed our breakfast and coffee and she went off to work, I went for the typewriter. I thought I would take a crack at an idea I had for another science-fiction adventure. I had been writing the other one for so long that it seemed strange not to be typing. So I started, and by the time she returned home, I had hidden about twenty pages under her pillow. The first one was very easy. It was simply a chronological recording of what actually happened to me. Now I was embarking on pure fiction, but I continued, mostly for her entertainment.

Bonnie came home around six. We chatted for a while and then got ready for our night out. Tonight we had decided to have dinner at Veronica's Ristorante. A cute little place, it looked like the stereotypical Italian restaurant. It was owned and operated by Vito and Veronica Abandonato. Vito was the cook. Veronica was the hostess. They had only two waiters, both older Italian men who spoke very broken English. But we always suspected they knew more than they let on. They wore white aprons with black shirts and never had time for small talk unless you could speak Italian.

The walls were decorated with pictures from the old country and the Abandonato family vineyard and home. There were family pictures of Don Abandonato and his large family and other pictures of Veronica's home and family, and the grand wedding pictures of Vito and Veronica. Veronica had been an absolute knockout in her youth, and Vito had been a large, muscular man when they married. They were a very lovely couple. Now in their midfifties, she had the body that showed her affection for pasta, and interestingly, he was very thin, and his jet-black hair had turned gray. No longer strong enough to stomp the grapes, Vito was one helluva fine cook. They were still quite a handsome couple and the nicest people you could ever meet. The always made us feel special when we were there, and Vito would come out of the kitchen just to thank us for coming to his humble, little place, as he called it.

The large main dining room was filled with round, wooden tables covered with red-and-white checkered tablecloths, and the long east wall displayed a wine rack filled with wine from the old family farm in Sicily. He had it shipped monthly and always had a few bottles of aged premium wine from very good years. Tonight, I was in the mood for linguini with white clam sauce, and Bonnie wanted the eggplant parmigiana.

We ordered quickly so we could eat slowly and still make the movie on time. Tonight it was an old movie, *Angels with Dirty Faces*. I had seen it a dozen times growing up. Now I would see it in the theater with my wife as a just-released film with the stars in their prime. In my time, most were dead or very old. But the great thing about movies was that your favorite stars stayed young forever. Cagney and Bogart were two of my favorites. The noir mysteries they starred in definitely had an impact on my interest in detective and police work.

There was something very special to me about seeing this movie in its own time, and I didn't mind driving to DC to see it. This evening would turn out to have special meaning for us in a way we hadn't anticipated. It seems that this was the screening in DC for this movie, and guess who was there to help promote the movie? None other than Humphrey Bogart himself. I couldn't believe it! Here was the star of the film alive and in person. This was a man who died in 1957 … *Oh my God, he doesn't know that in less than twenty years he'll be dead*, I thought. We were standing in line to meet him, shake his hand, and get his autograph. I wanted to tell him to stop smoking or he wouldn't have a very long life with Lauren Bacall, but he wouldn't know what I was talking about. He wouldn't marry for another seven years! Then I remembered Doc's warning about doing things that could alter the future. I shook his hand, got his autograph, and told him what a pleasure it was to meet him. We went back inside and took our seats.

Here I was with my wife, watching something that was brand new to her and very old to me. I enjoyed this movie on that night more than ever before. After the movie, we walked and talked awhile before we returned to the car and headed home. We thought it was a great surprise to see Humphrey Bogart, and still another surprise awaited my bride when we got home.

As she pulled back the covers, the pillow moved just enough to reveal the paper-clipped pieces of stationery beneath. She smiled and eagerly picked it up and began reading. Once again, I waited anxiously for her to finish and give me a critique. Once again, she liked it. Now I was certain she was just being kind. I kissed her in gratitude, and she returned it with passion … end of discussion.

Weeks went by, and my writing became sparse, and each night when she looked for that day's edition, she was disappointed when there was nothing. What I didn't know was that I would soon get an unbelievable surprise.

It was now summer, and the weather was wonderful. My boss was happy with my work, and things were okay, but I longed to be back in my detective role and decided to talk with Bonnie to see what she thought of me trying it here. I wasn't sure what her reaction would be, and I certainly didn't want to add stress to her life just because I was bored at work. I rehearsed my speech on the subject, and when I returned home from work that evening, I was ready. If she had the dayshift, I was usually the first one home, so I retrieved the mail, walked through the front door, and tossed it on the dining room table as I headed to the fridge for a cold beer and to drop my lunchbox off on the kitchen counter.

As I walked back past the dining room table, I casually stopped to sift through the mail for anything of interest. The third letter down was addressed to Bonnie with the return address of Harper and Brothers, publishers in New York. I thought it must be junk mail and set it back down. I went upstairs to change and clean up. I heard Bonnie come in, and I had just started down the stairs when I heard her scream. I jumped the rest of the stairs and ran to her, thinking something bad had happened. When I reached her, she was sitting at the dining room table, laughing.

She looked at me and jumped into my arms, still laughing.

"What is it? What is it?" My curiosity was piqued.

She kissed me and then pulled away and handed me the open envelope. I read it quickly. It was an acceptance of my manuscript, a contract, and a check for one thousand dollars! Being the sharp detective that I was, it didn't take me long to figure out what she had done. The manuscript I had joked about writing, the one she encouraged me to write, the one I did write as a way to remember all of my two lives, and the one I had thought was stuck on a shelf or in a drawer somewhere in the house and had been forgotten, wasn't. She had obviously, unbeknownst to me, sent that manuscript to one or more publishers. Those actions of hers had led to what she received in the mail today, which was about to change my life forever.

I stood there dumbfounded as I stared at the check and the contract. Not only had they bought my book for one thousand dollars, but the contract also said I would receive a 5 percent royalty on all book sales, and if I signed this contract, they would pay me a five-hundred-dollar advance on my next book!

I asked Bonnie where she had put the second manuscript I had puttered around with but never finished and hadn't worked on for some time. I remembered she said she thought it was also good, but back then I had thought she was just being kind. After all, I was a cop, a detective, and a time traveler, not a writer. How could this be? However, I was not one to question honest money, so I signed the contract, marked the spot to write another book, and put it in the mailbox. I signed the check over to Bonnie and told her to put it in her savings account.

"No, sir, I will not. I will put it in our household checking account, and you can now quit that job you dislike so much and concentrate on that second book. Besides, you know I got a nice raise last month, and that will help even more."

I could tell that she was serious, and this was nonnegotiable with her, so I just agreed, picked her up, and spun her around as she shrieked, and when I stopped spinning her, we had the longest kiss, which simply caused us to skip dinner.

The next day, I called my boss and asked him how much notice he would like, to which he responded none, as he had two guys waiting for an opening. I thanked him for giving me a job and said I had enjoyed working with him. When he asked why was I quitting, I said I was now going to write novels, and a publisher had picked one I had written to publish. I told him I would give him a signed copy. He told me he was sorry to lose me, but he wished me luck and said he looked forward to reading my book. I was happy we parted on good terms.

My career as a machinist was over, and my new career as a writer was starting today. Actually, it had already started thanks to my wonderful wife. I felt like the guy who had just won the sweepstakes on the first try. After all, what did I know about writing? All I had done was record a true event that happened to me. Someone once said truth was stranger than fiction. My true event would never be believed, so I called it science fiction, and bingo—a published novel.

Over the next few months, I received some letters telling me what to expect and that once the book was on bookshelves, I should hopefully receive royalties. Meanwhile, I pulled the typewriter back down from the bedroom closet, picked up with where I had left off on the second story, and started banging the keys.

Within six months from the day I accepted the check from the publisher, I started receiving the royalty checks. They were small at first, but over time they steadily grew. Not too shabby. They were not enough to live on but enough to improve our standard of living a bit. Not long after that, my book was on some best-seller list and was also being distributed overseas and translated into six other languages. I sent them the second book, and soon I received another contract.

I was able to write about things I knew about that hadn't come to pass, and within the fiction genre, they were widely accepted by the public, much to the happiness of my wallet. My books were based on things I knew from the future—a future that was really my past, a life that now seemed like a giant dream. I leaned back in my chair and wondered if my books would somehow change the future. Maybe some great fiction writer from the future wrote like I did, but his or her books would never catch on because I had taken from the future to create a writing personality. Would that stop this person from becoming successful in his or her time? Would he or she have to resort to a life of crime and rob a convenience store, killing a pregnant woman and thus preventing the birth of a child who would have become some great person who went on to do some great and beneficial thing for mankind?

I leaned forward in my chair and chuckled to myself, thinking I was placing far too much importance on my literary skills, and continued typing.

My idea for book number three was about a young man from a wealthy family who became president and was assassinated in a motorcade under circumstances never totally accepted by the public. Maybe I would take it down one of the conspiracy theory avenues as opposed to the conventional thinking. Didn't want it to be too close to the truth. People might begin to wonder about me and get the wrong idea. Know what I mean?

The holiday season of 1939 came and went. Bonnie and I celebrated the New Year. It was now 1940. We were in our second year of marriage, and I was happier than I had ever thought possible. Doc's blunder had turned out to be good for both of us. He got his Sheila back, and I had Bonnie. I was no longer angry with him; in fact, I owed him a debt of gratitude. I now had an identity and a job and had pretty much forgotten the other life and was enjoying this life. Bonnie was a good and decent woman, and a better wife no one could find.

Certainly my life would turn out much differently than I could have ever imagined, and Julie, who had been a major player in that life, was gone from me forever. But now with Bonnie, I would be happy until my dying day, and you couldn't pay me to return. That was not to say that had I returned to my time as planned I would not now be married to Julie. I truly loved her then, but my life had changed when the plans failed. I had been lost at first. But fate, luck, God's will, or something put Bonnie and me together, and nothing could change that now. Bonnie provided me all the happiness one could ever hope to have. See, I now understood that it was no longer about me; it was about *we*.

Nineteen forty brought us another year of happiness, another novel took off, and I was becoming a sought-after author. This one cost the publisher three grand, and royalties began almost as soon as the book hit the shelves. Books one and two were also still paying off, and there was scuttlebutt that book one was being looked at by moviemakers. The year slipped away quickly, and soon we were celebrating the holiday season and our second anniversary. I remembered looking at the calendar Bonnie brought home, replacing the one for 1940. It was now 1941. I flipped to December and circled day number 7, the date that America would never forget. I wondered what it would feel like to live during this time. Little did I know what horror would befall me, starting with one day in the future, a day and a time I had studied in school.

CHAPTER 21

DISASTER STRIKES

December 6, 1941, was a Saturday much like any other Saturday, only I was sick to my stomach and couldn't eat. I knew the country would go to bed that night and wake tomorrow to the horrible news on their radios. I tried to sleep but couldn't. Neither could Bonnie. She knew through me what was to happen. We sat on the couch in our pajamas, listening to the radio, waiting for what would soon become history. I drank coffee. I didn't want to sleep. Bonnie nodded in and out of sleep but refused to go to bed when I suggested it. I remember how that night seemed like it would never end. But finally the sky lightened as the sun was beginning its climb out of the ocean. It would be approximately five more hours before the first wave of newscasts come rolling in.

Then it happened, just as I had told Bonnie it would: December 7, 1941. It was followed the next day by President Franklin Roosevelt's speech that contained those famous words, *"a day that will live in infamy."* Bonnie and I discussed it and cried about it as the first reports rolled in. Secretly I think she hoped I was wrong. Secretly I had been wishing that saving Sheila had caused the war not to happen. Her mom called, and friends called, all wondering if we had heard and how this could happen.

We listened to the radio from the first broadcasts that came in until the day tuned to night. A few days later, we declared war on Germany as I had predicted. We were both saddened by the amount of human lives that would be lost, lives that would be torn apart. Bonnie loved me, but she was a healer. She resisted at first, but each day as she heard the reports and saw young men climbing aboard trains and buses and heading to boot camps, her guilt of not helping reached the breaking point.

Almost a year had passed when finally one morning she told me she could not bear the guilt of not helping and could no longer resist the call to help, particularly in a time of crisis. I selfishly tried to talk her out of it. When I exhausted all my reasons for her not to go, I finally admitted that I understood.

She enlisted in the military as a nurse and an officer, and of course was quickly sent overseas to Britain to help the wounded Allied forces. She wrote almost every day. I stayed at home for a while, but all I could think about and worry about was Bonnie. It was driving me crazy. I had never missed anyone so much in my life, either of my lives. I was like a dead man who forgot to lie down, a zombie. I couldn't take it anymore.

I had served in the marines during my time, and I now had enough phony identification to get a job; in fact, I did such a great job creating a person, I got a draft notice. I was told by letter where and when to show for a physical to see if I was fit for military duty. I did, and of course I passed. They sent everyone who passed to a large room to wait. Later, we were informed that we had passed and would soon be receiving orders by mail to show up at some army recruit depot. However, prior to receiving orders, we were certainly able to join another branch if we were so inclined.

Of all the branches of the American military, the marine corps was always the place I would serve. I took care of all the loose ends and pending matters. Two weeks later, I went to the marine recruiting office in Alexandria and signed up. If I was going to serve, it would be as a leatherneck not some dogface. However, I made one really bad miscalculation. In fact, it never crossed my mind until boot camp that the marines didn't go to fight in Europe. They went to fight in the Pacific. Oh God, what a blunder for me. I wanted to be in Europe to be closer to my wife, maybe even be close enough to see her, but that would never be now. I would be halfway around the world from her. I was too deep into the system for them to let me change.

I was happy about being drafted for two reasons. First, I had too much time on my hands, and that time was spent being miserable. Second, I felt terrible about not doing my part to fight the enemy while my wife was doing her part. We would both be gone three years, and I had to survive for her, to be with her again. That was my goal. I was going crazy replaying in my head over and over our last conversations and our lovemaking. I missed the feel of her soft skin under my fingertips, the scent of her body, and the look in her eyes when our bodies were united, the way she held me like she would never let me go, and the soft, loving words she spoke to me in our most intimate moments. It truly was enough to take my sanity. Dear God, how I missed her. But now I wouldn't have time to dwell on the thoughts that drove me out of my mind. I would be fighting for my life.

I knew from sports and life that when you tried to play it safe, that was when you got hurt, or in this case maybe died, so I fought with reckless abandon. I killed more than my share of enemy troops and was wounded twice but in neither case badly enough to be sent home. It did get me two Purple Hearts, and I was awarded the Congressional Medal of Honor. My closest call came on February 19, 1945. I was part of the American forces that invaded the tiny island of Iwo Jima to secure airstrips for American B-17 and B-29 bombers.

We called that island the Gray Pork Chop. We learned later that we had encountered approximately twenty-one thousand of those well-entrenched Japanese defenders. It took us more than a month of fighting over an inhospitable terrain to dig out and overtake the Japanese. When the guns went quiet and the battle ended on March 26, 1945, as many as seven thousand of my brethren were dead, and another twenty-four thousand were wounded.

While almost seven thousand of my fellow marines died there, only about one thousand of the twenty-one thousand Japanese defenders were captured alive. B-29 crewmen subsequently used Iwo Jima as a safe haven during their three-thousand-mile bombing runs to Japan. Later in history, I would be told that their gratitude to the marines was immeasurable.

I was there that day and guarded a small band of marines who raised our flag on top of Mount Suribachi. I couldn't tell those brave marines that day that a photograph taken of them raising Old Glory would later be cast in bronze and stand on a hill overlooking Arlington Cemetery and Washington, DC. The only portion not cast in bronze would be Old Glory herself, but it would carry the real stars and stripes and be bathed in lights every night and wave in the light of day for every American to know what those who had gone before them had sacrificed for them to remain free. I was never more proud. In fact, whenever I see those well-known photos, I get all choked up with pride and sadness. Pride for how we fought like tigers for our country and sadness for the men I knew who paid the ultimate price for our freedom.

On the next island we hit, I was one of the first to get wounded. This time it got me a ticket home. They said I had eaten enough Japanese lead for one fellow. They patched me up and sent me back to the United States, and the VA hospital got me put back together. In less than a month, they released me, and I finally walked—I should say limped—into our home.

I was home but still not cleared to work. I tried to do some writing, but worrying about Bonnie zapped my ability to concentrate. So I mostly listened to the news about the war in Europe and wrote to her. I mean, I knew when it would be over to the day.

I lived for letters from Bonnie. They came fairly regularly, and when a few days went by without one, I would worry myself sick. Then I would let out a great sigh of relief when the next one came. She often talked about how busy they were when heavy casualties came in.

The end of the war was drawing near. I knew German troops were dying by the thousands in the dead of the Russian winter. The Allies were pounding Germany, and our troops had penetrated their borders and were rolling toward Berlin. I hadn't had a letter for a few days, and I woke one Saturday to loud knocking at my door. I thought it might be Joe, the mailman. He would often knock when a letter came from Bonnie, especially if he hadn't brought one in a few days. Or could it have been Bonnie, home on leave. Or it had been a year; maybe she had been sent home for good! I ran to the door in hopes that I would see her standing there.

CHAPTER 22

STRANGE VISITORS

I pulled open the door with great enthusiasm. I saw her … smiling at me. But it was a mirage, as she vanished before my eyes, and instead of my Bonnie stood two soldiers. They were in dress uniform, with somber faces. One started to talk, but I didn't hear a word he said. He didn't have to tell me. My worst fear had just come true. My heart sank as I took what he handed me, closed the door, and proceeded to cry like a baby all that day. My Bonnie, my wife, was gone. The ironic part was that Saturday, the day I learned of her death, was April 7, 1945, one month and one day before VE Day. The day the bloody Nazis surrendered to the Allies and the Allied Commander Dwight David Eisenhower.

She had actually been killed three days before that Saturday, just a little more than a month before it was all over. Oh God, why Bonnie? Why did she have to stay on after the time she could have come home? Was it my fault because I was in the Pacific and she didn't want to be home worrying about me? I drove myself crazy with all the wondering. The irony of it all was that I knew all the notable things in history, but not the individual details. If only I'd had Doc's machine, I could have looked into the future and said, "Don't go. You will die for certain." Or I could have gone back and saved her.

If Doc hadn't abandoned me … I wondered if there was ever a chance of getting home. Should I start returning to the beam-out spot at noon and midnight? If I ever got back, I would have Doc send me back to save her. That helped a little. The reason I had stopped going there was because of my dear, sweet wife, but with her gone, there was a hole in my heart, and I started to get homesick again. Back in my time, I had many friends and acquaintances. Here I had mostly Bonnie, and that was all I had really needed.

Time slowly moved on, and every once in a while I'd have an okay day, but I would lapse back into tears and an immobilizing depression the next. It was so hard. Bonnie had rescued me, given me a home and a woman's love and comfort. She had given me the honor of being my wife. Then when her country needed her, she unselfishly answered the call. She did what so many had done; she paid the ultimate price for her country—her life. But I wondered how many men had been saved by her efforts. Her letters were full of the horror she had witnessed, the lives she and her team were able to save, and the long days and nights. Often they worked twenty-four-hour shifts as waves of wounded were transported to the field hospitals. Then that night when the enemy shelling hit her area, I only pray that she didn't suffer.

I volunteered to work for the war effort by day and came home at night … to an empty house. I knew both wars were about to end. The Germans and the Axis would sign an unconditional surrender on May 5, 1945, and the Japanese would do the same on August 15, 1945. It was great to see the world at peace again.

For most of the world, it was celebration time. Brave men and women from around the world had stopped evil madmen of that time. Nobody but me knew that soon America would be brought to the brink of what might have been WWIII, and a man named Kennedy would stare down our number-one enemy and turn him back, perhaps preventing it. However, this same man would be assassinated after sending advisors to another country ablaze with civil war, leaving a vice president to become commander in chief and to escalate that war and engage us in a bloody battle that would be fought by appeasing politicians instead of our military, thus rendering a costly defeat for us and leading to the senseless loss of American lives.

Many, like me, who were glad WWII was over now had to shake the horror and pain of losing a spouse, a son or daughter, or a parent. I was surviving, but that was about it. While I had made many friends in my life, they were all back in my other world in the future and had long forgotten WWII. I isolated myself somewhat, meeting only people I needed in order to function somewhat normally. Of course, there were Bonnie's friends with whom we had socialized a little, but we were both homebodies, preferring to be together, just the two of us. I had gotten close with her mom, a very lovely woman who I loved dearly, but she had died more than a year ago. Neither of us could get home for her funeral, although we had both tried.

Now there was no one to help, no one with whom I could share my grief, and no one to give me diversions. I had never felt so all alone in my entire life. I had loved only two women in my life, one in each lifetime. The irony was that I was in the time where that love was dead. I spent countless hours in my memories of both loves. If only I had the plans and specs for Doc's Teleporter. Then I could go back in time and save Bonnie. She had been so beautiful, loving, and so very romantic. Without her, it made nights almost impossible.

I often found myself falling asleep in my lounge chair, listening to the radio.

After one year, I was still struggling. I did finish another book during that time. It was a story about Bonnie and me, our meeting, falling in love and marrying, the tragedy the war brought, and finally her death. It was written as fiction, but I knew it was real. It was a romantic tale of love and loss that, surprisingly to me, became a best seller. My publisher invited— no, *insisted*—me to attend a huge book-signing event for this new novel, and I reluctantly agreed.

I was surprised at the turnout and talked with so many people who loved my book because they said it made them feel like they weren't alone in their loss of a loved one because of that rotten war. I was pleased that so many found it helpful. My publicist took me out for drinks afterward. We got a wee bit more than a little tipsy, and she seduced me, or that's how I preferred to think of it. She told me afterward that she had wanted to be with me in that way for some time. By the time she told me that, I felt like I had betrayed Bonnie even though I wasn't doing anything wrong.

I left, telling her it could not happen again, but in less than two weeks, we were together again. We began a relationship that lasted about nine months, and then she wanted to get married, and I just stalled and stalled until one day she informed me that if I wouldn't marry her she would find someone else … and she did. I cared for her but not like I had for Bonnie, and therefore I couldn't ruin both our lives just to keep from being lonely. She remained my publicist, and we went back to a professional relationship. I even attended her wedding but skipped the reception.

From there, it was one woman after another. Some lasted only a few weeks, others maybe a few months, but no one could replace Bonnie. It was like drinking water but never curing your thirst. So, I had someone to keep me warm at night and give me moments of delight and guilt afterward. I felt Bonnie would understand my need, but I believed she would not forgive me for marrying someone else unless I loved her as much as I did Bonnie. I always felt that Bonnie was close to me and that she watched over me, but if I truly loved another, she would be gone, really gone. Yes, I knew that was probably silly, but I really believed that, and I lived accordingly.

Years passed, and I grew older and older, more tired with each passing year. It was now April 1953. Korea was the conflict that plagued the country now. I knew its end was only a few months away, but hearing the TV and radio news firsthand added to my depression.

Then another visitor came calling. It was on a night when I was in deep depression over Bonnie, the war, and the fact that I couldn't sleep. That's when Mr. Jack Daniels came to see me again after a long absence. I hadn't seen him since before I came to 1937 and met Bonnie. Isn't that a funny statement? Most people would say since they came to Washington or Chicago or some other place, and I said I came to 1937, which was the truth, but it just sounded funny.

He was very good company that night, and his numbing way seemed to help with the pain, but the next day, the pain of her loss required another visit from him. Soon he needed to stay with me all day and then tuck me in at night. One night he and I discussed Julie and my other life. He convinced me to go to the hotel at midnight to step on the infamous spot that should have taken me home so many, many years before. I explained it would do no good, but he insisted, so we waited until we had just enough time to be there by midnight.

"Okay, my friend. Here we are, and it is now time to show you the idiocy of this trip. I am standing here on the spot, and it is now midnight." I was a bit wobbly, slurring my words, and could not have given a shit less if I died right that second as I stood on that special place—a small piece of real estate covered in asphalt that I had visited many, many times in vain as the world as I had known it slipped further and further from my reality and a new one grew to take its place. After falling in love with Bonnie, I had never returned to this place until now. I was sure I wouldn't be there now if it had not been for the encouragement of my long-lost friend, Mr. Jack Daniels.

I laughed at him. "You know, Jack, this is a futile thing to do, but what the hell?"

I looked down at the cracked, black macadam surface. There was a small chunk of asphalt missing; that chunk always guided me to step on the right place. Even in my inebriated stupor, I recalled the times I had stepped there before and was transported through time, from my world to this world and back. And I was reminded of the fact that the one time it didn't work, my life was changed forever.

I had been given a new life. Some might say for the good; some might disagree. I ached for Bonnie and missed her terribly, but I really couldn't complain. God had a reason. Sometimes it wasn't clear. Sometimes a person questioned, "Why me, Lord?" But someday when the pain of her loss dissipated, it might become clear. Until then, Jack would help ease the pain if only on a temporary basis. I finished my pint, tossed the empty bottle on top of the trash in the Dumpster, listened to the glass break with a loud crash, and took a deep breath. I was about to prove to my friend Jack that I could step on this place and nothing, absolutely nothing, would happen.

It was at that moment that I heard someone yell, "Hey, mister. You there! What are you doing?"

I saw him walking quickly toward me. Hell, I didn't care. I was too damn drunk to care. I just looked down and slowly put one foot on the spot and then the other. I stood up straight and spread out my arms as if to gesture, *See, nothing happens.* Then when I had proven my point and was just about to step off that spot and walk away, I felt something. It wasn't the stranger coming at me and grabbing me. I knew this sensation. It was the sensation I felt each time I traveled through time, that very same feeling I first discovered while riding in the backseat of my father's Hudson as a youngster when he would traverse a vertical curve at a high speed.

The End ... never

Printed in the United States
By Bookmasters